Quickies – 3
A Black Lace erotic short-story collection

D1638239

Quickies – 3
A Black Lace erotic short-story collection

BLACK LACE

Black Lace books contain sexual fantasies.
In real life, always practise safe sex.

This edition published in 2007 by
Black Lace
Thames Wharf Studios
Rainville Road
London W6 9HA

Nothing But This	© Kristina Lloyd
The Game of Kings	© Maya Hess
Sonata	© A.D.R. Forte
Rush Hour	© Cal Jago
Number One	© Candy Wong
Cooking Lessons	© Teresa Noelle Roberts

Typeset by SetSystems Limited, Saffron Walden, Essex

Printed and bound by Mackays of Chatham PLC

ISBN 978 0 352 34128 0

Nothing But This Kristina Lloyd

I call him the Boy although he isn't. He's skinny enough, it's true – as skinny as the kids who do backflips in the square – and there's not a single hair on his flat brown chest. But his age is in his eyes, eyes as green as a cat's, and when I look right at him, though we're meant to be ignoring him, I see eyes that might be a thousand years old.

He's been following us for half an hour, weaving among the crowds, his flip-flops slap-slapping in the dust of the souk. 'Hey, mister! Hey, lady!' he keeps calling. 'You wanna buy carpet? Teapot? Saffron? You wanna buy incense? Come, come! Come to meet my uncle.'

His urge to 'come, come' sounds grubby and erotic and the refrain pulses in my head like some dark drumbeat, weird enough for me to wonder if it's going to bring on one of my migraines.

'Lady, you wanna buy handbag? Real leather! The best! Hey, mister, nice wallet for you! Look this way! You are my guest. Come!' The Boy averts his eyes, head down and spinning, and the whole song and dance routine seems a pastiche of the real hustlers, an empty act he can turn off at will.

No wonder he can't look at us: we'd see right through him.

'I feel like David bloody Niven,' mutters Tom.

Tom's posh as fuck, so self-assured and confident you don't even notice it. He's relaxed and ironic. A bit on the prim side, it has to be said, but I adore every hot salty inch of him. I like to draw him, standing, sitting, lying, sprawling, my futile bid to capture him in charcoal and pencils. In evening class, I learnt to draw not just the object but the space around it. I learnt to see absence. 'What's not there is as important as what is,' said our tutor, although personally I'd contest that with Tom. I'm quite a fan of what's there. Naked, he's pale and softly muscled with strong swimmer's shoulders and thighs like hams. Sometimes I sketch his cock, big and randy or just lolling on his thigh, framed in dark curls, and when I show him the end result he'll invariably wince. 'Oh God,' he drawls, looking away and sounding slightly camp. 'You're so *vulgar*.' But he can't help smiling and I know deep down he likes it.

'*Pssst!*'

It's the Boy. I can't see him, only hear him. The medina is crammed with noise, its maze of tiny streets choked with the scents of paraffin, leather, spit-roast meats, sour sweat, baked earth and strong rough tobacco. Here and there, the souk opens out, exposing its squinting stallholders to a livid blue sky. But for now we're in the thick of it, two clueless pink-skins in an ancient labyrinth, lost among beggars, hawkers, shoppers, mopeds, donkey carts and big wire cages squawking with heaps of angry hens. The Boy's hiss slices through the chaos, clean as a whistle, but I can't spot him anywhere.

I'm disappointed. I'm supposed to be relieved because the official line is he's been annoying us from the off, prancing around like some mad imp of consumerism, urging us to buy this, buy that, buy the other. The thing is, we do want to buy a carpet, a nice Berber runner for the hallway, but he's probably on commission and, besides, we'd rather do it in peace.

My disappointment tempers the arousal I'm half-ashamed to acknowledge. At first, I couldn't be sure it was sexual although I suspected it was. Heck, it usually is with me. And then I knew damn well it was when my groin flickered its need and I grew aware of my inner thighs, filmy with sweat, sliding wetly as I walked, my sarong flapping around my ankles. But it's a weird kind of sexual. It's not as if I fancy him, this slip of a lad with the calm, creepy eyes, but I'm drawn to him in a way I can't identify. He keeps dropping back from us to sidle among the crowd or prowl at a distance, elegant and stealthy, stalking us like prey. My money's in a belt. I must have checked it a dozen times. I don't think he's a thief though.

I don't know what he is. All I know is he's

sparked off in me some intrigue, some furtive hunger that makes me not quite trust myself. We keep walking, Tom and I, and within the humid fabric of my knickers, I'm as sticky and swollen as a Barbary fig.

'*Pssst!*'

His call sounds so close I actually look over my shoulder, expecting him right there, but no sign. It's as if he's invisible, some mythical djinni up to no good or a golem from the old Jewish quarter, laughing to himself as I pat my money belt once again.

'Seem to have shaken him off, the little shit,' Tom says mildly as he unscrews his water bottle.

I realise Tom's not hearing what I hear, making me question my senses. The heat in this place stupefies me and I haven't been sleeping well either. At night, after an evening of jugglers, magicians, fire-eaters and snake-charmers, the bedsheets tangle themselves around my legs, cobras for the pipe-player, and my mind whirls with madness and enchantments. To soothe me, I think of the stillness beyond the town: snow-capped mountains, endless deserts and a black velvet night sprayed with silver stars. But I sleep fitfully, slipping in and out of dreamscapes, grotesque and lewd, and I wake each morning sloppy with desire. When I sink onto Tom's cock, drowsy and heavy, I feel fucked already, post-coitally limp, as if I've been possessed by an incubus, a gleeful demon who screwed me senseless as I slept. My limbs seem to liquefy as I ride Tom, awash with vagueness, remembering feral creatures, how they pawed at my flesh, and priapic monsters with gas-mask faces, rutting in steamy swamps.

I don't imagine we'll buy a carpet today. I'm not really in the mood. Feeling a tad psychotic, to tell the truth. But I hide it well. I'm probably just premenstrual.

A few minutes later and the Boy's with us again. I don't see him but I smell him, a pungent sexual whiff as we pass stalls selling metalware, shards of sunlight glancing off pewter, copper and brass. Then, in the shadows behind, I see two green beads peering out from the gloom, points of luminescence, freakishly bright. My heart pumps faster. Among so many brown-eyed folk, those eyes are hauntingly strange, non-human almost. He doesn't belong to these people, I think. An outsider, perhaps; a man who leaps across gullies high in the Atlas mountains, surviving on thin air.

'Oh, God, there's that smell again,' complains Tom.

A few yards ahead, the Boy darts beneath a tatty awning. He's wearing filthy, calf-length shorts and his legs, I notice, are dark with hair. He's a youth, I think, and then some. Old enough, I'm quite sure, to go snuffling under my sarong.

'It's foul,' says Tom. 'Really fucking rank.'

I think he's talking about the Boy. I think he's

smelled his appetite and is repulsed. Then it dawns on me he's talking about the tannery. When we were last here, I was about ready to retch with the stink of it but now the tannery's just a backnote and it's the Boy's odour I'm getting. It's as if my senses are tuning in to him, to the sound, smell and sight of him, and everything else recedes. The whole thing's starting to make me nervous.

Tom offers me the water before taking a swig himself. He has beautiful manners, partly because he's from Surrey but stemming too from a naturally submissive streak he doesn't fully acknowledge. He's no pushover, believe me, but his gentle manner, combined with a curious intellect, makes him tend to the deferential or at least a fascinated passivity. Give him a good book and he's lost for hours. Give him a good woman – or better still a bad one – and he's lost for months. I took him away from someone else. Well, he left her for me at any rate. Two years down the line and we're still in love, half-daft and quite besotted.

But I'm no fool. I know damn well if some other woman caught his heart he'd be gone in a flash, leaving me spitting with rage. I like Tom a lot. I want to hang on to him. I want to keep him mine. But all I can do is hope for the best. And meanwhile, I try to catch him as I can, all those impossible charcoals and pencils, all that seductive permanent ink.

My favourite sketches are the ones I do in bed

at night, Tom lying there with his mouth agape, dreaming eyeballs quivering beneath his lids. I love him so much when he's fast asleep, when he doesn't even know he exists. Tom doesn't realise I do this. I keep the sketches well hidden, my treasured possessions, proof of all the hours I stole from him while I watched him sleep. I have bouts of insomnia, you see. It's not only out here.

'Half a mo'. Batteries,' says Tom. He edges past slow, swathed people, and I wait for him by a spice stall. Black strips of tamarind and threaded figs hang like jungle vegetation over sacks heaped with nuts, dried fruit, tea leaves and herbs. SNORING CURE – NEVER FAIL! says a sign and APHRODISIAC FOR THE KING! proclaims another. The air is powder-dry and colours catch in my throat, scarlet, copper, ochre and rust, an earthy rainbow of seasonings that makes me cough like a hag. 'I have medicine! Never fail!' cries a djellaba-hooded man, and I protest my health, realising there's some seriously dodgy shit for sale here: a turtle strapped to the canopy's scaffold, bunches of goats' feet, dried hedgehogs, chameleons, snake skins and live lizards flicking around in giant-sized jars.

'*Pssst! Lady!*'

His voice goes straight to my cunt. The sensation's so strong he might have tongued me there. My senses reel and I turn, catching a glimpse of sharp brown shoulder blades before he's swallowed up by the crowd. Across the way,

Tom's holding a pack of batteries, appealing to a stallholder who looks out with a half-blind gaze, his eyes veiled with cataracts. A woman with a wispy beard jostles me. Instinctively, I check my money-belt and I see the Boy just feet away, throwing a backwards glance, an invitation to follow. I cannot refuse him. I don't even question my options. I just go.

As I move, Tom turns. He catches my eye, nodding acknowledgment of my direction. It's fine, he's cool. He rarely makes a fuss. And, should we lose each other, we've both got our phones. An image comes to me of my mobile trilling away, whiskery rats nosing the screen where the words 'Tom calling . . .' glow for no one. I push the image away. It's not important. But the Boy is.

Anxious not to lose him, I squirm through the crowds, keeping his shorn head in my sights. A man with a monkey distracts me briefly and for a terrible moment I think I've lost him. Frantic, I whirl around, a vortex of faces blurring past me, colours racing. He's gone, he's gone. But seconds later, I have him again. I watch as he vanishes into an archway so narrow that at first I think he's ghost-walked through a wall. Panicking, I hurry, elbowing people aside. Somebody curses me but I don't care. I'm high with fear. I don't know why I'm following him. I only know I can't stop. Dark eyes flash around me, and my cunt's pumping nearly as hard as my heart. I'm in the grip of something scary, my juices are hot, and I try to remember if I've eaten something funny. Maybe I stood too close to those desiccated hedgehogs. God knows what they were for. God knows what I'm doing.

In the alley, I pause to catch my breath. I've got the Boy in view again. The alley's cool and white-washed, not much wider than a person, and a few feet in, the racket of the souk goes dead. There's no one around but us. Suddenly, it is so still. So silent. My own breath surrounds me, a whispering rush like a seashell to my ear. I walk on and yet I don't think I move. I just pant. The sun doesn't fall here, but the alley seems to shine with its own light, the white walls reflecting each other in a numinous glow, and I wonder if this is it. I wonder if I'm dying on an operating table, my soul sailing up to enter the kingdom of heaven, or to at least try tapping on its door. I want to look back to see where I've come from but my head's far too heavy. I can't turn.

There is nothing but this: me, my breath and the Boy. It's as if I've slipped into a chink in the world.

Several yards ahead, half-crouched, he creeps along with cautious grace. His slender torso is sweet and supple, the rack of his ribs visible beneath grimy fudge-brown skin. The scent of him drifts in his wake, pheromonal and ripe. Civet, perhaps, or musk. How pliant his body must be, I think. How smooth his skin, how eager his hands, how tireless those beautiful, plum-coloured lips.

I follow, both of us keeping a steady pace, then the Boy stops, poised low. His arched spine protrudes in a knobbly ridge and the stubble of his hair prickles with light. I freeze, feeling I ought to, and realise I'm barely breathing. Then, slowly, the Boy swivels his head around to face me. And that's when I nearly keel over. Because the eyes that look into mine belong to no man on earth. For several stunned seconds, I stare back. They are cat's eyes: green as gooseberries with black slit pupils.

Fear thumps me in the gut but I cannot scream. I cannot move either. I can't do anything. I just gawp, rooted to the spot.

He smirks and turns away. I think I must be in one of my dreams. Soon, I tell myself, I'll wake at the hotel and I'll straddle Tom's cock in a trance of remembering. I'll rock back and forth, head swimming with a post-human dystopia, a stinking medieval market peopled with DNA freaks or inter-species offspring. Look around and they all seem perfectly normal till you spot their webbed feet, forked tongues, folded wings or dog-fang teeth. And I'll climax and so will Tom. Then we'll get up, have breakfast, take a bus to a town with tiled palaces, koi carp and orange trees, and we'll buy something lovely in Spanish leather or cedar wood and everything will be all right.

The Boy creeps forwards. I'm so scared and I'm so wet. But wet is winning. I follow, turning a corner then another until he ducks into a small archway in the wall. Moments later, I'm there too, head down and heart hammering as I descend three worn white steps.

In front of me, a cool cavernous chamber opens out. Hung with tapestries and oil lamps, its edges are banked with stacks of carpets, and in a far corner stands a cluster of earthenware jugs alongside sacks of grain. Sunbeams, soft and fuzzed with dust, slant down from high plasterwork arches, a tranquil light for prayer. It smells of straw and mice.

I catch a glimpse of the Boy as he flits from one stone pillar to another then stays there, hiding. Sitting cross-legged on a tall pile of carpets is a bald, muscular man with dark skin and heavy brows, his jawline shadowed with bristles. He's bare-chested, whorls of black hair clouding his pecs and making a seam over his neatly rounded paunch. He looks like a cross between the Buddha and a thug. It's not a look I'm familiar with but I do like it. He has a small, neat smile, and he's observing me steadily, chin propped on his fist. I get the feeling he's been expecting me.

'Hi,' I say, trying to sound brave.

I walk deeper into the chamber, across the flagstone floor, shoulders back. I know this man is going to fuck me and, frankly, I'm ready for it.

No one replies. The man keeps watching me,

smiling. Though I'm still scared, I have an inkling of a new confidence. I'm starting to feel powerful and ageless, like some whore of the Old Testament. The Boy emerges from behind his pillar to lean against it, arms folded and smirking. His attitude's changed. He has the jaded, haughty air of a rent boy, hard faced and sleazy. It's attractive in a sick kind of way. His eyes are normal too. Well, relatively speaking. They are the most astonishing sea-green – *National Geographic* eyes – but they are normal in that they are human. I must have been seeing things earlier, a trick of the light, nothing more.

They both watch me as I sashay forwards. I feel deliciously easy. I'm a harlot, houri, concubine, slave. I could dance like Salome, seduce them with a strip show, except I don't have seven veils, just sarong, vest and Birkenstocks.

Besides, my guess is, these guys really don't need seducing.

'You chose well,' says the man, addressing the Boy.

Now hang on, I think. Didn't I just walk here myself of my own free will? Then I correct myself. Who am I trying to kid? I've been picked up, haven't I?

'My uncle,' says the Boy, grinning and nodding at the man.

Uncle tips up his chin in a curt greeting. 'Show her to me,' he says to the Boy.

Barefoot, the Boy saunters forwards. He parts

my sarong, exposing my legs, and presses his hand between my thigh. All the weight of my body is suddenly in my cunt, resting in that skinny hand. My gusset is damp and he paddles his fingers there, grinning at me before latching on to my clit. He rubs through the fabric, judging my expression. I want to appear impassive but the smell and touch of him makes me dizzy with longing. Truly, I can't remember ever feeling so horny. I guess I don't manage to pull off the cool, composed look because the Boy chuckles softly. In a whisper, he says, 'Ah, you like that, don't you? Hot little bitch.'

Well, you got me there, I think.

'She's OK, Uncle,' announces the Boy. 'Nice and wet.' He tucks the gusset aside then pushes two fingers up inside me. My knees nearly buckle. 'Really wet,' he adds, stirring his two fingers around. In the silence, I hear my juices clicking.

'Excellent,' says Uncle in a thick, languid voice. 'We have a willing woman.'

'A willing slut,' says the Boy, 'who wants to get fucked.' He seems to be relishing the words, testing their strangeness like an adolescent keen to rid himself of innocence.

I'm relishing them too. I like being objectified. It takes the heat off having to be yourself.

The Boy, still working me with his fingers, slips his other hand up my top. He strokes me through my bra before pushing up the cups to squeeze and massage. My nipples are crinkled tight and he flicks and rocks them, bringing my nerve endings to seething life. Then, just as I start to feel I'm losing myself, falling open to ecstasy, the Boy pulls away and crosses the floor to Uncle.

It's a cruel, desolate moment. I'm about to protest but before I can utter a word, the Boy has sprung up onto the carpets, leaping from a standstill like a mighty ballet dancer. On his haunches, he straddles Uncle who reclines, mouth parted, to suck on the Boy's fingers, offered like dangling grapes. The Boy cups the man's shiny head, supporting it, and Uncle goes slack with surrender, eyes closed in bliss, as he slurps and snuffles on a sample of my snatch.

Now, I'm not averse to a spot of guy-on-guy action but I've only just arrived and I'm feeling a touch neglected. So I walk towards them because, dammit, I want to play too. As I near, they stop their weird feeding and, holding the pose, look down at me with benign curiosity, blinking heavily. It's as if they've never seen me before. Jesus, it's creepy. Without smiling, they continue to stare and blink for what seems like an age. A pair of green eyes and a pair of bright brown ones.

Then Uncle perks up, his expression changing to a villainous leer. He looks seriously gorgeous, like he ought to be behind bars. Sneering, he sits straight, swinging his legs over the edge of the carpet-pile, and delves into the crotch of his baggy pants. His pants are slate-blue silk, and a materialistic impulse asserts itself because that's just the shade I want in the hallway. I consider asking for a thread so I can choose a carpet with a matching weave but the moment passes. I have a different object of desire, other needs to gratify.

'Suck my dick for me,' says the man, grinning. He releases a big fat erection, wanking it gently, the muscles of his beefy arm flexing under dark skin. It's a beautiful brute of a cock, arrogant and obscenely large.

'Dirty bitch,' adds the Boy. He still sounds like a kid trying out rude words. 'Suck the man's dick.'

I'm happy to oblige. The stack of carpets are almost shoulder height and all I need do is lower my head to engulf him. His pubes tickle my nose and, butting deep within my mouth, he's superbly stout and powerful. My head bobs between his thighs and I'm getting weaker and wetter as I dream how it'll be when this beast slides into me. The Boy drops to the floor and I feel him at my feet, nuzzling my ankles then crawling under my sarong. I spread my legs for him and feel him rising, the heat of him on my skin, his shorn, silky head, his tongue trailing a path up my inner thighs. He pulls down my knickers and I feel him between my legs, his hot breath on my cunt before his tongue, so delicate and perfect, dances over my clit and squirms into my folds.

Oh, my. That tongue has truly been places. Like his eyes, it could be a thousand years old, a tongue that's pleasured geisha girls, ladyboys and

Babylonian whores. Fingers fill my cunt, a thumb rubs my arsehole and moments later I'm coming hard, gasping around Uncle's cock, Uncle clutching my head, keeping me steady for fear I neglect his pleasure in favour of my own.

'She's a slippery little bitch, isn't she, huh?'

Uncle's voice is loud enough to carry across the chamber. He's talking to someone else; not to the Boy, and certainly not to me. I pull back and turn, wiping saliva from my mouth.

Tom, of course. Hell's teeth, I'd forgotten him. He's standing within the white stone archway, looking somewhat dazed. Really, I'd completely forgotten him, forgotten the man I love. Well, I guess fresh meat can do that to a girl.

Tom stares, mouth sagging dumbly. I worry for a moment, fearing my blue-eyed boy is going to be appalled, but I can see he's interested, absorbing the scene. It's that fascinated passivity again. 'My God,' I can almost hear him say. 'You're so *vulgar*.'

'Come, come,' cries Uncle, jumping down from the carpets. 'Welcome, my brother!' He pumps Tom's hand and claps him on the shoulder as if they're the best of mates. 'You want her to suck your dick too, huh?' Pleased with himself, Uncle laughs over-loudly.

I think Tom's had a hit of whatever I've had, the scent of dried hedgehog or something. He smiles. I know exactly what he's going to say. He's going to say, '*I* don't mind' in that sing-song way he does when I say, 'Shall we have coffee here or there? Rice for dinner or pasta?' It can get a bit annoying, to tell the truth. He looks at me; his smile's ironic. '*I* don't mind,' he says, and I realise he knew that I knew he was going to say that, and his tongue's in his cheek because he knows all that knowing will amuse me. Long-term relationships can be so nice.

The Boy, on his hands and knees, peeps out from under my sarong to edge a cautious pace forwards. Then he's motionless, watching as Uncle leads Tom to a low bank of carpets, stacked at three levels like a shallow flight of steps. A hazy shaft of sunlight falls across them, revealing tiny squalls of dust as the men clamber and sprawl across this wool-woven stage. Uncle sits on the higher level, legs akimbo, and Tom lolls within his silk-clad thighs, head resting there as he yields to an off-centre shoulder massage. Uncle bows forwards, murmurs in Tom's ear, and Tom smiles gently, stretching his spine in a discreet arch, his pleasure private and contained, as the man kneads with big oafish hands.

I stand there, entranced, hardly able to believe what I'm seeing. The Boy edges closer, moving gingerly as if wary of disturbing them. Sitting back on his heels, he watches intently as Tom relaxes deeper in to the massage, occasionally grunting.

When Tom and I fuck, a glazed expression sometimes settles on his face. His eyes close, his mouth drops open, and he looks completely gone, blanked out with bliss as I move on top. He's got that slightly dead quality about him now, and when Uncle reaches forward to remove his T-shirt, Tom acquiesces, raising his arms, as docile and obliging as a sleepy child. He doesn't even protest when the Boy pads forwards to nuzzle his pale chest. All he does is smile fondly and, like a basking chimp, he stretches his arms back, exposing their white undersides, tendons taut, his dark patches of armpit hair attracting the Boy who tentatively sniffs, a hand sweeping broad caresses over Tom's flexing body. Tom is clearly loving it.

Well, you sly old tart, I think.

I can't take my eyes off him. I wonder if they've drugged him. And then I'm clearly not thinking straight myself because soon I'm wondering whether it actually *is* Tom. Perhaps someone – or something – has got inside his body because I've never seen him like this before. Tom likes to size up situations, to tread carefully, to fret unnecessarily; and he's never shown even the slightest interest in men. And now look at him, pushing the boundaries of his experience as if it were a walk in the park. I start to fear I may never get him back.

But then I notice his smile fading and he moistens his lips, a small moment of nervous desire. It's exquisite, so tender and Tom-like, and I feel I know who he is again. I see his Adam's apple bob in his throat and, in his neck, a hint of tension, as he tests the air for a kiss. The Boy bends over him, their lips meet, and lust flares in my groin. I watch a knot of muscle shifting in the Boy's jaw, movement in Tom's neck, and I'm all eyes as, without breaking the kiss, the Boy reaches down to unzip Tom's fly. Tom's erection springs out, weighty and lascivious.

I don't know what I want to do most: watch or join in.

Then Uncle grins at me, rummaging around in his silky blue crotch. He exposes his cock and moves it against Tom's face, tipping it back and forth like a windscreen wiper. 'Come here,' Uncle says to me. 'Bring us titties.'

He's dead right: I want to join in. So I cross to them, whipping off my top half as I do so. Greedy and urgent, I scramble up onto the carpets and Uncle welcomes me by holding out a brawny arm. He opens his mouth and I fill it immediately with soft pink breast, pressing a hand to his crisp chest hair, my body pushing against the bulk of his belly. His tongue lashes my nipple and he delves under my sarong, searching eagerly for my hole. With a force that makes me gasp, he plugs my wetness with thick, crude fingers. Grinning up at me, he holds my nipple between his teeth and gently pulls on it, stretching my flesh. I hold his gaze, daring him to keep right on going.

For the first time, I notice how stunning his eyes are. They're a hard amber brown, sparkling like topaz. But this is no time to be romanticising, because the guy's moving us into position, my sarong and belt are off, and I'm utterly naked, poised above that prodigious cock, buttocks split in his big rough hands, cunt wide open. With heavy luxury, I sink down on him, groaning all the way until I'm stretched and stuffed to capacity.

Truly, it's a beautiful moment, made more beautiful by the fact that beside me is Tom, being sucked off by the Boy. They're both naked too, Tom with his knees apart, the Boy's shorn head bobbing in his crotch, his pert little butt stuck up in the air. Sprawled against the carpets, Tom has an arm flung wide, eyes closed, mouth open. I've never seen him looking quite so dead. I wonder if his expression's the same when I go down on him. My guess is not. All the same, I try and commit that face to memory, thinking maybe I can reproduce it some time in charcoal and pencil.

Tom must sense me looking because as I start to slide on Uncle's cock, he reaches out with a blind hand to stroke my arse. In that tiny affectionate gesture, I feel such a connection with him, such warmth. And I feel free to fuck like there's no tomorrow, knowing Tom and I are united, mutual support in mutual depravity; for richer, for poorer; for better, for worse.

Uncle clasps my hips, bouncing me up and down, and I'm as light as a doll in his hands. This man can do what he wants with me, I think. And I don't mind if he does. It's a while since I've been overpowered. The two of us mash and grind, silk hissing beneath me, sweat forming on my back where sunlight heats my skin.

'Hey, brother,' calls Uncle, addressing Tom, 'does she like it in her ass? Huh? A big prick in her tiny little asshole?'

Tom's too zonked to reply immediately. He just sprawls there, half-dead, before his head rolls sideways, eyes still closed. When he finally speaks, it sounds as if it's costing him an enormous effort. 'Probably,' he croaks.

The Boy pulls away from him. Tom groans in despair.

'Dirty little slut,' says the Boy excitedly. His cock is ramrod stiff, its ruddy tip gleaming, and against his scrawny frame it looks grotesquely large. He springs off the carpets, takes a small copper can from near an Aladdin's lamp, and pours thick clear liquid into the palm of his hand. 'Uncle,' he says, 'you in her pussy, me in her ass. Bam, bam, bam. We fuck her hard, yes?'

Uncle laughs lightly.

'No,' I whisper. Then louder: 'Yes. God, yes.'

The Boy leaps back onto the carpets, lubricating his cock with lamp oil. Tom groans again. I reach out, feeling sorry for him, and Uncle, gent that he is, shuffles us closer. I lean over to kiss Tom and he responds eagerly, our tongues lashing awkwardly as Uncle pounds into me. Sweat dribbles down my back into the crack of my buttocks and I feel the Boy's greasy fingers press against my arsehole. He wriggles a finger past my entrance and I'm groaning into Tom's mouth as the Boy opens me out, forcing the ring of my muscles wider, making me slick and ready.

'Keep her still,' urges the Boy, and Uncle obliges, his cock lodged high.

'Lean over,' orders the Boy and I obey. His knob nudges my arsehole and pushes into my resistance. I think I'm going to be too small for him, my other hole too full, and that it's all going to hurt like hell. I make a feeble cry of protest.

'Don't pretend,' snaps the Boy. He grasps my hips then there's a flash of pain and, with a sudden slippery rush, he's fully inside me, and I'm swamped by dark, fierce pleasure. Uncle calls out triumphantly. I feel I'm on the brink of collapse, the intensity of having both holes packed so solidly taking me to a place I didn't know existed. I gasp into Tom's mouth, quite beyond kisses now, as the two men start to drive into me. Bam, bam, bam, as the Boy said. I have to pull away from Tom. I need air. I need to groan and wail.

Beneath me, Uncle's face is flushed with exertion. He spots me looking at him and he grins, meeting my eye with a deliberate gaze. There's the weirdest kind of friction going on inside me, the two men jostling my body as they fuck. And then I know I've lost it. I know pleasure has reduced me to lunacy because I see something wild in Uncle's eyes. His pupils contract and, for a moment, they are like the Boy's: bright with black, slit pupils.

It's the light, I tell myself, the light, the light. And I can't bear to look. I flop forward onto Tom, seeking a kiss, wanting the reassurance of his mouth, his nose, his face. I'm close to coming and so is Tom because the Boy, gorgeous greedy creature, is sucking him off again. As the two cocks shove fast and hard inside me, I nudge my clit and then gasp into Tom's mouth, our lips so hot, so wet and loose: 'I'm coming, I'm coming.' That sets him off and he groans and pants, his body twitching as he peaks. My orgasm rolls on and on, and Tom is still gasping into my mouth, still coming. It feels sublime, orgasm-without-end. Our lips slide and smear, and nothing else can touch us. It's as if we're melting into each other at every breath. And I am him and he is me, and we are all ecstasy, all delirium, all gone.

Sex, I think, will never be the same again.

We didn't buy a carpet for the hallway that holiday. But sometimes it's like that. You go out hoping to buy one thing and come home with something totally different. I've stopped drawing Tom in the middle of the night as well. I don't feel the need any more. I don't have that yearning to capture him. Because I have my Tom, I have him entirely, from now until the end of time. And if I ever start to doubt it, I just need to picture his face, glazed with rapture at the point of climax.

He doesn't know what he looks like. I don't know what I look like either. People don't, generally speaking, do they?

All I know is that he'll never look at another woman like that; he'll never be able to. Because when he comes, something shifts in his eyes. He rides the wave, annihilated with bliss, the two of us breathing so hard and so deep. And when he looks at me, his beautiful blue eyes have black, slit pupils. And I am him and he is me. And I know we are possessed.

Kristina Lloyd is the author of the Black Lace novels *Darker than Love* and *Asking for Trouble*. Her short stories have appeared in several Wicked Words collections.

The Game of Kings Maya Hess

Tessa drove her sweating horse down the field for the final time that day and clipped the ball with her mallet, sending it at an acute angle into the goal. The handful of onlookers sent a few casual claps her way before ambling back to the clubhouse, most of the other players and spectators having already retired to the veranda for pre-dinner drinks and talk of the impending matches.

Tessa was the last player left on the field and, as she guided her horse back to the stable yard, she again noticed that strangely familiar figure leaning against the perimeter fence, one foot cocked on the railings, both hands gripping the top bar. Tessa knew he'd been watching her throughout the afternoon's practice sessions. In fact, he hadn't taken his eyes off her from the moment she'd arrived at the club earlier. She didn't understand the man's interest in her, especially as she was caked in sweat and dust. Tessa had an uncertain feeling that she knew him from somewhere and guessed that he recognised her too.

'Last off the field. Does this mean that you're dedicated or apprehensive about tomorrow's play?' The man stepped away from the fence and positioned himself in front of Tessa's exhausted horse. The creature threw back its head and snorted indignantly.

Tessa brought her leg across the rear of the saddle and slipped lightly off her mount. Mandarin-coloured dust erupted around her black leather boots. She raised her eyebrows, allowing herself a beat to study his face, to harvest any recollections about the man before she spoke.

'Dedicated, of course. Apprehensive, never. My entire team is honed and ready.' Tessa offered a terse smile but wasn't sure why her voice hardened and her jaw clenched. She found herself tipping back her head and bringing her knees together in almost military style. She clicked her mouth and walked on, holding her horse's bridle.

The man remained by her side. 'Jack Wentworth,' he said, again positioning himself in the horse's path and this time sending it into a series of frustrated whinnies.

Tessa patted its shoulder and gripped the bridle. His name was vaguely recognisable but Tessa's impatience of the man's rudeness outweighed her desire to know who he was. Doubtless she'd heard his name mentioned at another match. He was evidently a Polo player, dressed in jodhpurs and team shirt and cap.

'I have to get Nitro back to the groom. He needs water and rest. Excuse me.' Again, Tessa urged her horse on and headed across the arid yard to the stable block. Even though the sun was teetering on the horizon, the temperature was still in the high eighties and the humidity was unbearable – quite different to the tepid English summer she had left a couple of days earlier. Orange and gold fingers spread from the sunset and stretched over the distant hills, illuminating the far-away clouds like brightly coloured saris. Tessa was aware that the man was following her and, as she gave Nitro to the stable boy, she felt a hand in the small of her back steering her towards the clubhouse.

'You look thirsty. Come and have a drink with me.'

Tessa was annoyed. She was exhausted, dirty and needed to collect her thoughts in readiness for tomorrow's game but nevertheless allowed herself to be guided to the clubhouse veranda, driven simply by intrigue.

Seated at a table underneath a gently ticking fan, Tessa enjoyed the feeling of sweat evaporating from her face. She allowed her head to drop back on to the soft padding of the cane chair and let her eyes fall shut. All she could hear was the pounding of her horse's feet through the dust and the thwack of mallet on ball in the day's relentless heat. The practice sessions had gone well and she was sure that her all-female team would easily hold their own in the initial games of the tournament.

Jack Wentworth soon returned with two tall

gin and tonics and unexpectedly seated himself directly next to Tessa on the small Colonial-style chair.

'You don't remember me, do you?' He took a long draft of the icy drink and plucked out the chunk of lime. Jack was sitting with his elbows resting on his knees, his upper body angled round to confront Tessa.

She stared hard at his sun-browned face and noticed his southern-hemisphere accent. She drew upon all her remaining resources to place him but simply couldn't. The way his face broke into a series of laughter lines around his white teeth stirred something within Tessa but she finally convinced herself that she was merely responding to his fierce good looks. She shrugged and picked up her drink. 'Sorry, I don't.' She didn't want to flatter the stranger with too much interest and so gave more thought to sipping her drink and admiring the sunset.

Jaipur was certainly a stunning place and, as if he had read her mind, Jack Wentworth interrupted her thoughts. 'Indian sunsets are like no other in the world.' He gestured towards the west and the accumulating cirrus clouds hanging over the distant hills. 'There's a storm brewing. Tomorrow, maybe the day after.'

'I don't think so,' Tessa said, thankful for the change in conversation. 'I've heard that the –'

'Melbourne 2001. Our team won, yours lost. We got the prize.' Jack Wentworth's clipped tone coupled with the look of absolute triumph and smugness he now wore as he sipped his gin and tonic shattered any feelings of tranquillity or enjoyment the sunset held for Tessa. The man was clearly trying to suppress his laughter.

'Melbourne ... prize?' Tessa stammered. How could she ever forget *that* match? Simply the worst game of Polo her team had ever played; totally and utterly the most humiliating three days of her life. After leading her team to defeat on the field during the mixed-team match, she then had to lead three of her best players to the beds of the opposition. Having made the bet with the cocky, self-assured captain of the all-male over-35s team, it would have been dishonourable not to keep to their side of the bargain.

Tessa wasn't sure if it was shame or an involuntary reaction to the memory that caused her top lip to curl into a smile as she sipped her gin. The memories filtered back like the gathering clouds on the horizon. She recalled agreeing to such outlandish sexual frolics because she hadn't known any of the men in the room and had convinced herself and her teammates that they would never encounter any of them ever again. It was an anonymous orgy – a sweating mass of nameless bodies hungry for their prize and never to be seen again. But here he was, Jack Wentworth, veteran Polo player, veteran gambler and, if it was truly him four years ago in that hotel room, then expert lover too.

'I barely remember it,' she said, almost choking on her drink.

As if sent by the gods, an Indian boy interrupted the pair with a tray of fresh drinks and a dish of spiced nuts. Tessa took a large mouthful of her drink and closed her eyes for a second. Suddenly, she felt something fiddling with the top of her breast and recoiled, sloshing gin and tonic on her jodhpurs.

'A mosquito was about to crawl down your shirt.' Jack held up the insect and burst it between his finger and thumb.

'Gosh, you're brave,' Tessa said, reaching for a handful of nuts.

Jack gripped her arm and pulled her even closer. 'You were the best,' he whispered in her ear, his breath hot and spicy from the snack. 'I had a go with the other girls but, if you remember, we finished up together for hours.' Jack continued to crunch in her ear. 'Look, you're all wet.' He made to wipe the spilt gin from Tessa's inner thigh but she swatted his hand away.

'It was nothing to me. A casual fuck with a bunch of strangers. We were simply honouring our bet. And no, I don't remember you especially. It's all long forgotten.'

'Really?' Jack smirked. His pupils dilated and his breathing deepened.

Tessa noticed the dew of sweat across his forehead and top lip, somehow magnifying the roughness of his face and similarly the country from which he came. This lot were a tough team and Tessa knew they were in for a hard ride when they played the mixed games tomorrow.

'Hold still again.' Without considering the tenderness of her breast or even that her nipple had drawn up into an angry peak, Jack flicked the back of his hand across the front of Tessa's grimy shirt. 'Little bugger was after your tit.' A flash of white teeth again as, instead of plucking off the insect, Jack firmly took hold of Tessa's upturned nipple and refused to let go, even when she shifted uncomfortably.

'I'd like to make another bet with you.' He kept a firm grip on Tessa through her shirt. 'And given that you're so confident about your team's ability you needn't be worried. But if you should lose to us then, well, we'll see.' Jack smirked at Tessa's near inability to speak. But words weren't necessary. There was an unspoken agreement between them as palpable as the looming storm.

'Like I said, my team is –' Tessa grimaced and fought the sudden stab of heat that rocketed through her lower belly and between her legs.

'Your team is what?' Jack laughed as he rotated the nipple between his fingers. His body concealed Tessa's increased writhing from any onlookers, although he wouldn't have cared if anyone had seen him tormenting the woman's sensibilities.

'My team is up for any hollow bet you may toss our way, Mr Wentworth.' Tessa begged her body to be still because, with every uncomfort-able twist that she made, the wretched man pinched her further. Shamefully and unable to suppress a large moan, her back suddenly arched and her head dropped back on to the cushion. She simply did not know if this was nice or not. The fire between her legs told her one thing and the pain in her breast told her quite another. She had an enormous desire to touch each end of her body, thrusting her flattened hand between her legs to build up the tiny pulsing waves as her unfolding lips blossomed from within her tight jodhpurs and also an infuriating desire to press Jack Wentworth's gin-drenched mouth firmly around her burning nipple. She did neither.

'It's not the rest of your team that we want. It's *you*. Tell me it's game on.' Jack was serious, his face reflecting the pleasure that only one half of Tessa was enjoying.

She abruptly swung her head away and took an eyeful of the bulging disc of fire as it finally dismissed the day and dropped out of sight below the horizon, turning the Polo field, the site of tomorrow's battle, into nothing more than a dull patch of brown wasteland.

Mustering all her inner strength and pride, Tessa wrenched herself free from Jack's grip and stood up, convinced that every other person seated on the veranda could feel the heat radiat-ing from between her legs. 'Oh, definitely game on, Mr Wentworth. Prepare your teammates for a thrashing.' Tessa added a satisfying whine to the end of her speech, mimicking Jack's heavy accent. 'When we win, I will take pleasure in flaunting what you can't have. Melbourne was a one-off. It can never happen again.'

Tessa left the table and heard Jack laughing as she walked away. She felt his stare burning her arse as she pressed through the crowded club-house and vowed that, despite the now incessant tingling in her knickers, she would fight to win tomorrow.

She'd hoped that she'd be alone in the hotel room. God knows, she *needed* the room to herself and was overcome by a wave of disappointment as she saw her teammate step out of the shower as she entered the small suite. Any privacy was out of the question.

'Boy, was I ready for that.' Sophie winked as she allowed her towel to drop to the floor. Judging by the pink glow on her skin and the skim of silver juice on the tip of her clit, Tessa figured that she'd done more than wash in there. 'It's those damned Australian players.' Sophie wiped her hand across her brow in a dramatic display of approval. 'I'm going to have to disappear to the loos after each chukka tomorrow. What with this heat, being in the saddle all day and those horny buggers from Down Under.' Again, she swiped her brow but stopped when she saw her filthy and worn-out captain. 'Hey, what's up with you?'

Before Tessa replied, she suddenly felt relieved. Sophie was right. It wasn't Jack Wentworth who had made her feel so horny, causing all rational thought to frazzle with the desire for sex. As usual, a day in the saddle, the relentless pounding from the well-worn leather had sent her level of desire and need for immediate relief spiralling out of control. Coupled with the heat and humidity, the exotic colours and smells of India, Tessa's senses were on fire. She couldn't wait to delve beneath her jodhpurs and find what awaited her. She just wasn't sure what to do about Sophie.

Tessa fixed a drink for them both from the mini-bar and settled on top of her bed, trying to gather the energy to shower. She watched as her unabashed and naked friend stood in the full-length window of their first-floor room and stared out at the twilight city beyond. Sophie sipped her drink, the only barrier between her and passers-by being the thin whiff of voile that billowed in the evening breeze, occasionally offering a glimpse of European breast or thigh to anyone lucky enough to be looking up.

Tessa took her chance. She couldn't wait any longer. Trying hard to obliterate her encounter with Jack Wentworth and the undeniably tough Polo she and her team would face the next day, Tessa raised her hips from the bed and slid her jodhpurs down her legs like she was peeling off skin. She knew she didn't have much time while her friend's back was turned and so, after hooking her panties aside, she drove two fingers up inside herself while her thumb beat against her saddle-ravaged clit. She was thankful when Sophie continued to gaze out of the window and began to talk about the day's events. It covered the mess of sound that came from her drenched pussy, literally like the floodgates had been opened now her jodhpurs were removed.

Tessa was only able to answer her friend in broken sentences and breathy gasps. She could hardly stand her fingers on her juiced-up lips, let alone when she caught the blossoming tip of her clit with her thumb. The temperature between her legs was surely a good ten degrees higher than the rest of her body, and as she worked on herself she caught a whiff of her own sweet musk mingled with saddle soap plus the reek of night-time Jaipur flooding in through the open window.

Another few seconds and Tessa was unable to prevent the hot rod of orgasm from choking her sex in strong waves of contraction, surging up into her belly, her breasts, her shoulders and throat. And it was only another second or two before Sophie finally turned from the window and saw her friend lying supine, several fingers still resting between her swollen lips, virtually passed out on the bed.

'Those Aussies get you all hot too, huh?' Sophie giggled and began to dress for the evening's social events. Slowly, Tessa pulled out of her delirious and exhausted state and realised that Sophie was staring at her sodden panties. 'I said, did that delicious team from Down Under do that to you, too?'

Tessa shook her head a little before pulling up her jodhpurs. She knocked back her drink, a frown creasing her brow. 'No, of course not. In my experience, they're uncouth convicts without any morals, on or off the Polo field.'

Shortly afterwards, when Sophie had dressed and vacated the hotel room, Tessa pondered just how serious Jack Wentworth had been about his wager. With the consequences of a defeat firmly in mind, Tessa stepped into the shower and began to work herself up all over again.

The heat was more intense than the previous day, despite the absence of sun. The distant cirrus clouds had matted to form a rosy-grey blanket of steamy cumulus that swelled and churned overhead. The conditions cast an eerie light over the Jaipur Polo Club as team captains from around the world gathered in the clubhouse. The afternoon's sport was set to include four games of mixed-team play, which was until recently a relatively unheard-of occurrence in the traditional and ancient game.

When Jack Wentworth tipped his cap and grinned in her direction from across the clubhouse, Tessa ignored him and ushered the rest of the Ashlea Ladies Team outside to the veranda. She wondered if Jack had been right yesterday about the impending storm. Certainly the sky was fleshed with layers of dense cloud and the air itself seemed to be saturated with anticipation. Tessa briefly looked to the skies and prayed for the rain to hold off. A downpour and a sodden pitch would certainly thwart the game against the Australian team, and in turn would scupper the result Tessa desired.

'Right, girls,' she announced, gathering them around her. 'Here are our tactics for today's play . . .'

The Ashlea Ladies won their first game against the female team from the USA six goals to four. Tessa urged her horse back to the stable yard, her expression a tight knot of anticipation and excitement. Tides of sweat and salt decorated the horse's black coat and, instead of allowing the stable boy to attend to the animal, Tessa set about cleaning him up and feeding him herself. She found the action therapeutic, despite the perspiration that poured off her own body as she worked hard to groom him. He would need several hours' rest and a big feed before the afternoon's game against Jack Wentworth's team. Tessa filled up Nitro's feeding trough to the brim and left him to rest.

The first chukka of the game against the Australian male team was a resounding victory for the Ashlea Ladies. Tessa scored a goal within three minutes of play, her mallet dangerously skimming the kneepads of Jack Wentworth as he thundered past trying to block her shot. She smirked as he pulled his horse around, a patina of sweat already visible underneath his face-guard. Tessa spoke softly to her horse as she steered him centre field again, patting his shoulder. Nitro was nervous and filled with unta-med energy, fuelled and eager like his owner.

Sophie and the other two women supported their captain as the game continued but, within minutes of play resuming, Tessa could see that a win against the male team would be near imposs-ible. Nitro was behaving devilishly, not at all like the highly trained animal she knew. Before she could think further about tactics, the Australian team scored a goal and when Tessa protested that there had been a foul she was slammed into silence by the umpire. The horn sounded and the teams swapped ends and during the next chukka two more goals were scored against the Ashlea Ladies.

Within three more chukkas, Tessa could see that the game had become virtually irretrievable and, in under an hour of play, the Australians rode off the field in victory seven goals to one. Tessa led her frenzied horse back to the stable yard, a dangerous glow decorating her cheeks.

'You girls go back to the clubhouse for refresh-ments. I'll settle the horses.' She patted her team on the backs as they trudged by, saddened by defeat. 'Tomorrow's another day and another match,' she offered as consolation.

Instead of attending to the horses immediately, Tessa tethered them and dropped down into a pile of fresh straw. She was exhausted and closed her eyes, allowing the straw to engulf her aching body. She wrapped her arms across her chest and was considering the delicious consequences of losing to Jack's team when she was suddenly startled by his resounding voice. She sat upright and took a moment to focus on the sight before her. Standing against the bruise-coloured sky in the stable doorway were the four members of the Melbourne squad. Each wore full uniform, including their boots and spurs, and firmly gripped their Polo whips. They formed an indomitable barrier, the sight of which sent Tessa's heart into arrhythmia.

'Prize-giving ceremony,' Jack announced with a smirk, stepping forwards from the group. Tessa made to stand but Jack easily lowered her back into the straw with one hand. 'Uh, uh. You're not going anywhere until we get what's ours.' Jack tapped his crop against the side of his boot.

Tessa hung her head, showing her shame for having lost and, in spite of her humility, she felt all her peripheral muscles tighten, sending a surge of heat and tension to the pit of her belly and beyond. 'I understand,' she said. 'You deserve your prize.' She sat limply and waited, while adrenalin seared her veins.

'Take off your shirt,' Jack ordered, distracting Tessa's gaze with a sharp thwack of his riding crop against the dusty leather of his boot.

Tessa swallowed and did as she was told. She crossed her arms and pulled the hem of her red and blue team shirt over her head. Instantly, she felt a breeze on her sticky skin but this was overshadowed by the heat coming from four pairs of eyes. Her full breasts, choked within her sports bra, were being studied from all angles by the other three players. Jack seemed untouched by the sight of her bare skin and sent the tip of his crop flicking across the sweat-soaked patch of white cotton between her breasts.

'Get that off too,' he said, disdain lacing his words, although Tessa detected a shudder in his voice.

She fumbled with the catch behind her back and allowed her bra straps to fall forwards. Before she could remove it completely, Jack had the leather end of his crop hooked under a strap and pulled the plain garment off completely. Tessa's shoulders instinctively drew inwards as her large breasts fell free but, when she saw three looks of approval from the others, she leant back on her hands and sank into the deep straw in order to better display her naked breasts. Her raspberry-coloured nipples had contracted to tight pink discs and her pale English skin was shimmering with sweat. Tessa waited with both fear and excitement as the other three Australians drew up by Jack's side. The men were clearly straining beneath their jodhpurs, the combined amount of eager cock a both frightening and delicious prospect for Tessa, who had now dropped completely back into the scratchy straw. She was surrounded by the team, with Jack very much in control of his players as he told them to flick and tease her with their crops.

'Take everything else off too,' Jack ordered.

Tessa could barely co-ordinate her fingers as the whips messed with her nipples and mouth. She managed to slide off her sturdy boots before lowering her jodhpurs to her ankles. It was always a relief to get them off, like shedding skin. The new layer of virgin flesh underneath was ultra-sensitive, maddened by every touch or breath of air.

Before she knew what was happening, Tessa was aware of Jack's riding boot easing her body back down into the straw. He deftly pulled the jodhpurs from her ankles and took a moment to appraise what had been revealed. He stood at her feet and looked back up her lean body, his gaze delayed by the tiny white triangle of thong at the top of her thighs.

Judging by the growing bulges in the team's tight-fitting uniforms, Tessa knew they approved of what they saw. Her lips and cheeks flushed with excitement and she felt like she'd pee herself if they didn't take her soon. But Tessa wasn't going to let them know how she felt. No, that was her secret and, while she lay meekly in the straw, she felt her skin explode into a thousand tiny prickles at the thought of shoving her neat little mound towards the nearest mouth.

Fighting back her powerful desires, wanting to make the game last for ever, Tessa watched timidly as Jack and his three friends stripped off their team uniforms. Like an aphrodisiac weather front, Tessa was overcome by the powerful but sexy stench of pheromones and sweat as clothes were discarded. One by one, sheets of tanned skin stretched over hard-working muscle were revealed to her disbelieving eyes. The other three team players were fairer than Jack, their naked chests dappled with autumn-coloured hair over sun-bronzed skin, and they were so similar in their good looks that they could have passed for brothers. Tessa was suddenly faced with three stiff cocks bursting from their prisons and the thrill that they were all hers nearly caused her to orgasm immediately. She raised her hands out of the straw in an eager attempt to pull the nearest one to her but Jack swiped her arms away with his crop.

'Not yet,' he barked and then turned to the player who had taken first defence on the Polo field. 'Lick her out but don't allow her to come.'

'You're the boss,' he replied, his face breaking into a grin.

Unable to protest even if she wanted to, Tessa

felt her ankles being gripped and drawn apart as she lay in the straw. The nameless Australian glanced at her briefly before getting to work. With his face close and his breath moist on her skin, he hooked a dusty finger inside Tessa's panties and drew them aside. The half-growl, half-moan he emitted assured Tessa that he approved of her neat and trimmed mound. She was certain that her clit would be straining between her swollen lips as if begging to be licked first. She hoped that he noticed and didn't waste any time. Maintaining the timid charade was becoming increasingly harder as her lust grew more urgent. She struggled violently against her body's needs as the first velvet stroke of tongue slowly drew up the entire length of her creamy pussy, sending her mind cascading into oblivion. All her senses merged together and battered her brain with unreliable signals. Overhead, she could see Jack looming, waiting, his stiffness growing ever bigger, keen to claim his prize.

The Australian's tongue felt huge and invading, like an independent creature set loose as it worked deftly on Tessa's sex. The fire that raged between her legs was somehow linked to the thoughts in her mind, and while she had often fantasised about sex with many men since the time in Melbourne, she never thought it would happen again. Tessa let out a wistful whimper as the realisation nearly drowned her. She lifted her hips from the straw and ground her sex into the man's face, like her swollen lips were a drooling mouth suffocating him with kissing.

'Get her to suck you off,' Tessa heard Jack say, although in her delirious state she was unable to put meaning to the words until she felt something warm and smooth and meat-like brushing against her mouth.

'Come on, sweetie. Open wide.' The voice seemed detached from the hard lines of his perspiring body as the Australian teased her mouth with his straining erection. It was the salty bead oozing from the tip that caused her to part her lips in order to taste it, leaving just enough space for the cock to push and ease itself between her teeth. The silent stranger held up Tessa's head and slowly manoeuvred his statuesque erection into her mouth, almost immediately having to fight against ejaculating down her throat.

'Steady, steady,' he growled, digging his nails into her shoulders.

Instinctively, Tessa pushed her fingers into the space behind his balls and began to circle the tacky patch of hairless flesh, causing the Australian to moan and sway as he levered his cock skilfully. He was sitting astride her chest, his buttocks brushing against the pale rise of her breasts, blocking any view of whatever was going on between Tessa's legs. But she was aware that something was happening, a changeover perhaps because the pattern of licking slowed and became firmer, and whoever it was down there was nibbling and biting at her clit with their teeth. She strained sideways, peering out over the top of the wide prick that was a millimetre away from choking her and saw the top of Jack's dark head between her legs. The other teammate, who had got her so wet initially, was now standing and looking a little lost alongside the fourth player. Jack must have sensed this also because he snapped a command at them.

'Don't just stand around. Make yourselves useful.' Jack beckoned them over. 'Get to work on her tits.' The lower half of Jack's face was smeared with Tessa's juices as he spoke and a low snarl could be heard as he buried himself once more between her engorged lips.

'You take that side and I'll have this one.' The raised clipped tones of the Australian's accent preceded the burning sensation that suddenly surrounded each nipple. Two unfamiliar mouths sucked and chewed noisily on her breasts, which somehow seemed to complete the electric circuit that was sparking throughout her body.

Moments later, Jack hauled himself upright as if he had surfaced from a long swim under water. His eyes were half-closed, perhaps because he was drunk on the juice drooling from Tessa's little pink sex, and he barely managed to give out further orders to the team through a gravelled voice.

One by one, the men dragged themselves away

from their positions and rearranged according to Jack's wishes. Tessa had no say in matters as she was roughly lifted and repositioned in the straw. She felt something warm beneath her back and when she sent her hands to investigate she realised that she had been put on top of Jack, her back covering his front so that she could feel his searing hot prick straining between her buttocks.

She felt his breath on her neck as he spoke. 'Ever had it up the arse before?' Jack was barely in control of his voice and the words came out as urgent staccato. Tessa shook her head as someone lifted her legs at a right angle to her hips and held them up high by the ankles. 'Ever had it up both before?' Jack let out an irrepressible laugh and took each of Tessa's breasts in his hands like they were handles for the impending ride. Tessa suddenly felt another mouth eating her sex and quickly working its way down to her exposed arse.

'No, of course not!' she insisted, her whole body now a mass of trembles and anticipation. The fear of what she knew was coming coupled with the pleasure of having her tight little arse exposed and prepared by a stranger was nearly enough to send her unconscious but she held on to the remaining shred of reality as her hips were lifted and her buttocks separated further by the remaining team player. Jack's thick cock nudged her little wet hole from underneath, while the other three Australians guided and pressed her down. She gasped as the tip probed her by a centimetre. Once Jack had found his target, he instinctively moved in mini-thrusts to gradually work the rest of his hungry shaft inside Tessa, lowering her on to his stiffness by pushing down on her hips. Eventually, it went in completely, causing Tessa to emit sharp moans as he moved.

'I want more,' Tessa wailed, surprising even herself as Jack powered home. 'You –' she pointed at one of the players '– fuck me now!' She already had her fingers pulling on her needy clit simply because she couldn't wait. Gone were her reservations and fake coyness. Tessa wanted them all in every part of her.

'I'll never fit in,' he said, eyeing Tessa's neat little sex with adoration. But he lowered himself on top of her anyway, jamming Tessa in between the two men like a sandwich filling. His cock soon found her swollen lips and gradually sank into her extra-tight pussy. With Jack pounding from behind, there wasn't much space left within her slim hips so the two men vied for space, eventually finding a rhythm that quickly brought each of them to the brink of orgasm and drove their shared lover to that critical peak of ecstasy.

Tessa stiffened, unable to comprehend anything at all except for the extreme feeling of fullness radiating from between her legs. As she was gasping for breath, turning her head both to the left and right, she was suddenly met by the remaining men's veined pricks competing for her mouth. Excited by the two different smells, Tessa lavished equal attention on each, offering a few slow and deep sucks to one before doing the same to the other.

The man on top of Tessa pumped her diligently, the stem of his cock grinding against her clit, before finally sending her catapulting inescapably into cascades of pleasure as her orgasm gripped and kneaded the men inside her. Pinwheels of ecstasy shot throughout her body to the very tips of her fingers as her sex contracted time and time again. Seconds later, both men were unable to prevent themselves from coming deep within Tessa's soft pink flesh. Their bodies went rigid above and below her as they were lost in their own feelings for the few seconds it took to empty their balls.

Tessa began to laugh. Aftershocks rippled within as her heart steadied and her open mouth suddenly became the receptacle for the other two men's hot and curdled ejaculation as they frantically pumped their cocks above her face. She was almost choking on the stuff as the tepid, salty liquid erupted over her in irregular bursts. Her tongue whipped around her lips to lap up the delicious mess, while the sensitive and softening pricks bobbed together mere millimetres away from her searching tongue.

'Allow me to help you,' said the Australian above Tessa, his semi-hardness still inside her. He dropped forwards and kissed her sopping face, cleaning up the milky puddles. Tessa was drenched and exhausted; she had been filled up to bursting point but was simply the happiest she'd ever been at losing a game of Polo.

As five exhausted bodies gradually relaxed and peeled off one another into the straw, Tessa heard thunder resonating in the distance. Moments later, fat bulbs of rain pelted the dusty ground outside the stable, slow at first but then with the urgency of a land that hadn't seen rain in months. The relief in the atmosphere was obvious. Jack had been right about the looming storm.

'So what went wrong with your game?' Jack asked above the noise, hoisting up his jodhpurs. 'You played like you were riding an unbroken colt.'

Tessa paused before replying, a girlish grin emerging beneath the sticky residue around her mouth. 'That'll be the oats I fed to Nitro earlier. They're guaranteed to drive him wild, making him virtually impossible to control.' She shrugged and picked up a crop, tapping it gently against her thigh. 'But it got me the ride I wanted.' She smirked naughtily and lay back in the straw to watch the lightning.

Maya Hess is the author of the Black Lace novels *The Angels' Share* and *Bright Fire*. Her short stories have appeared in numerous Wicked Words collections.

Sonata A. D. R. Forte

The notes of a piano sound over the drumbeat of the rain, plaintive and primal running together, falling and fading. I adjust the volume down, just enough that I can hear it without drowning the song of rain patter. Then I turn from the stereo and go to the sofa, where I sit and curl my feet under the warm velvet of my skirt. I can see nothing through the downpour. Water obscures the world outside, washing it away while I look out from this refuge of glass and latticework. Piano and rain.

I run my fingers along the windowpane, following the path of the rain. Lean my head on the glass and close my eyes, slip back into the semi-sweet place of memory.

It was pouring then too; a summer thunderstorm full of thud and bluster, the air pungent with the smell of rain. I'd sought shelter in a doorway, leaning against the dirty red brick wall in an effort to stay dry even though the wind still did its best to spatter water into my refuge. I didn't mind the rain, not much. Eventually I'd make the mad dash for my car and get there soaked and out of breath;

turn the heat on full blast while I tore off damp scarf and jacket and ruffled my hair up cockatoo style. But for now I was content to stay dry until the worst of the downpour had vented.

And then I heard Mendelssohn. Trio No.1 muffled by concrete and brick, audible only in bits and starts over the drone of rain, the splash of car tyres in puddles and the screech of brakes. I went still. Listening.

Somewhere within the building a door squeaked, banged. Voices murmured. Yet still the music carried on, unfaltering. Tireless and fluid with the ease that comes from true passion for the craft. It wasn't until the side of my head began to hurt that I realised I was straining to hear with my ear and cheek pressed against the damp wood behind me.

I thirsted for that sound.

The hallway looked like the inside of every other campus building once I entered. Struggling fluorescent tubes that lit dingy concrete once painted beige. Creaking wood floor and greyish-brown linoleum. The musty smell of ancient carpets and filing cabinets.

But the sound of the piano pulled me on, drew me in past rooms and offices filled with dusty instruments, scribbled-upon whiteboards. Occupied by grey, colourless people who typed or talked, oblivious to the emotion bleeding through the tired hallways with every note.

I walked past them. How could they not hear? How could they remain so insensible, pacing through life like this? Like horses with blinders, trotting past open fields; never seeing or knowing what they were missing. Never thinking about what could be.

The piano answered me, indifferent to anything but its own joy and its own wild pleasure. *Appassionato*.

At the room itself I halted outside. I wanted the music and what it promised: the careless longing, the sensuality. I suddenly didn't want to see the player, just another miserable human eking out an existence except for this one instance of unrestrained joy. So I leaned again against the room doorway and listened.

I let the music beguile me, charm and whisper to me of golden damask sheets, of pillars twined around with vines, of red velvet and wine-sweet kisses. Of those aching, powerful moments of feeling that happened too few and far between the stretches of ordinary life. A look or a smile in the aftermath of sex. An unexpected touch. An instant of understanding without words.

There in that fusty little building with the mouldy ceiling lowering at me, I knew desire. And then it ended. Left me like a lover urgently called away. Chagrined, I bit my lip and frowned at the ceiling.

I told myself I should at least thank the piano player. He or she might be just a humdrum little person, ignorant of the voice and the longing in the music, but I could still show gratitude. A little moment of kindness on my part. So I pushed away from the wall and turned to enter the room. And found my way blocked.

He looked down at me and we said nothing at first, for there was nothing to say. I'd seen his face before, across impersonal, busy spaces among too many people. Somebody not part of my world. Somebody I had no reason to make part of my life, even though I had looked and looked again at that face: long proud nose and full mouth. Dark, rebellious waves of hair. Eyes the pale green of ivy leaves.

Now I looked full into his gaze and I spoke, and brought him into my world. 'I heard your playing.' I didn't add that it was lovely, that it was rapturous. That it was any of the hundred foolish, mindless compliments I could have uttered. And he understood.

He smiled and lifted the fringed edge of my scarf; let the silky, woollen strands glide through his fingers. Hands like pale ivory, but with no hint of fragility. I was caught by that sudden, unlooked-for touch, netted like a stray fairy in a wizard's garden, and I should have known then any chance of escape was lost.

'I'm lucky you did,' he said and let the scarf fall.

Such intimacy and such arrogance, brazen in his defiance of convention. But since he had stepped out onto thin air and dared me to follow him, I did. I took his arm as if we were old friends. We left the building, careless of the stinging rain that fought for our attention with each cold gust of wind. Now there was no reason to hurry. I wanted to savour the minutes and the rain chill and his warmth at my side.

We found a café; spent hours talking over something. Coffee, sandwiches. It didn't matter. What mattered was his hands rubbing my wrists, his thumbs covering mine before tracing the lines on my palm. His pulse warm against mine. His green eyes and his smile.

But he didn't kiss me that first night.

We circumvented each other for a long, wasted time, keeping our interactions chaste because we could rise above things like animal desire. All we needed was the meeting of like minds. We wanted nothing but long conversations and tranquil silences.

We shared confidences and thoughts and books. Traded recipes for stuffed mushrooms and chicken pot pie. He taught me how to make English trifle, and when my custard didn't set and I fretted, he laughed and fed me strawberries. We drank all the sherry, ate the entire bag of walnuts and stayed up until morning.

I listened to his fears and he listened to my frustrations. He played for me while I sat beside him and listened, my head on his shoulder, my eyes closed. We promised each other that was how it would remain between us. Never would we fall into the trap of wanting too much.

There were promises to others: expectations and plans we could not simply throw to the winds.

'Never,' we said.

We were so stupid.

But he came to me first, after an evening of too much wine and too much poetry. After hours of meaningless social pleasantries; of mingling and smiling and small talk about nothing. Of listening to the party's hostess read Neruda while we pretended not to notice each other. Ignored the heat when we stood too close. I told myself it was the alcohol, the crowded room. Told myself it was anything but his eyes following my every movement, or the way he looked at me and smiled for no reason at all.

He took me home and stayed, shrugging off his jacket and hanging it up in the closet as if it belonged there. Letting the dog out and then coming to find me where I stood, arms folded, beside the darkened garden windows. Always that's how it was. I can look back now and see that I was ever the one to pull away first. To run.

Yet that night, when he rested his head on my shoulder, slipped the straps of the evening dress down and kissed the hollow just below my shoulder blade, I yielded without a thought.

'I've looked at you all night. I've wanted you,' he said.

I nodded, unable to answer, and he kissed the pulse beating in my neck. He cupped the dark-rose satin dress over my breasts and stroked the flesh through it. My nipples responded to that steel-ivory caress and rose to meet it, wanting more. I was his instrument and his art, craving his touch. Craving him.

I turned and pulled his mouth to mine. I kissed him and stopped halfway though, confused. There was no demand in his response, no bid for power. Instead, I felt him relinquish control; all that he was and felt and knew into my keeping. He gave himself to me that night.

Hard cock. Hard, tensed muscle in his legs. Soft hands. Soft skin on his thighs, his stomach, his ribcage: everywhere that I touched and licked and sucked. Naked and offered up for my taking.

I made him suck my fingers and ran them – still wet – over the head of his cock. Stroked it. He licked the tangy drops of his own arousal from my skin before I slid my fingers into him, and then I caressed him from the inside while I teased his cock with my tongue and my lips. He cried out with pleasure and arched his hips upwards, fighting release.

'I want your wet pussy,' he said. 'I want to fill you.'

'You will, love,' I said. 'Be patient. You will.'

I fucked his ass with my fingers and I sucked

his sweet cock until he came, thick and hot on my tongue, and then I licked the sweat from every inch of him until he rose again for me. He had his wish then, filling me and stroking my breasts, my neck, my shoulders while I knelt over him, my hips moving with his rhythm. And I wondered through a haze of orgasm and joy why I had ever, ever thought I didn't need him this way.

That first night. Such magic. Every night was magic, every morning and afternoon and instant of time I was in his arms. It was the times in-between. When we worried about who was watching and what they thought. Disapproving glances. Curious, harpy stares from those who styled themselves colleagues and acquaintances or, worse yet, friends.

I glowed when he touched me, but I cringed when others saw it, when I saw their lips curl in mockery or disdain. I didn't understand envy; I was too ashamed of my own unruly weakness. We both were.

Only the music tore away barriers. Listening to him play in the hot, navy-shadowed dusk, I closed my eyes and forgot the outside. I forgot reputations, and the now obsolete romantic attachments that still clung and brought twinges of guilt. I didn't think about the wasted expectations and the gossip left in their wake.

While he played, I was inside the music. The raw notes left me tired. Only his playing could pare me down like that, and strip away my pretences. His playing. And his fingertips on my skin.

Until the last day. It should have rained that day. There should have been skies of steel with an icy wind or perhaps russet, falling leaves whispering of loss. Something poetic. Instead we had humid air, muggy with the aftertaste of smog. Traffic and lines at the airport. Tasteless coffee in green and brown plastic cups with white lids.

He sat quiet, drinking his coffee and watching the planes inching by beyond the windows. Not sulking, merely accepting when he knew any more opposition was just a waste of time. He reached out, touched my shoulder, his eyes focused on the lace at my collar as if he contemplated an unfamiliar instrument.

'I'll miss you.'

Simple. Stated without guile or motive. Just a fact.

I looked up, trying to seem brave and matter of fact, trying to hold back treacherous emotions. 'Yes. And so will I. But . . .'

His fingers moved to cover my lips. 'You don't need to explain it any more, love. I already know.' A sad smile. 'I hope you're right, I hope it gets better with distance.'

The intercom pinged. We listened to them call my flight for the last time.

'It will.'

* * *

But even now, here in this house that still seems strange to me, I find that neither time nor distance has healed the wound. I was wrong. All I thought I knew turns out to be nothing.

A space of silence while the CD changes. A click before the music picks up again, filling the emptiness. Mendelssohn. I lower my head onto my folded arms on the back of the sofa. I don't want to see the rain. I don't want to remember. I don't want to hear those chords, stirring the ache inside, the futile longing for kisses and knowing fingers. I am too strong to cry and too proud to pick up the phone. So I sit here with only the sounds of piano and rain.

And then I hear the muted snick of the front door, opening and closing. I did not lock the door. This place, a little town in a distant country, doesn't warrant locked doors. Amazing, I think, that such a place should still exist. I look up, expecting to see a neighbour, or maybe the vet's girl with the week's prescription. But instead my heart leaps and somersaults like a schoolboy on the first day of summer. Even though I cannot command a single other muscle to move.

He stands in the doorway, raindrops caught in his hair and on his clothes. We look at each other, saying nothing. I, because I think he can be nothing more than a figment of my imagination. He should be a world away. It's where I left him.

He walks forwards, staring at me with such intensity I don't know whether I want to run away and hide, or let myself be pulled into the storm promised by that icy green gaze. He sinks to the floor at my side, rests his cheek on my thigh, and closes his eyes. A penitent and a pilgrim come through fire and trial, overcome at the shrine for which he has so long searched.

His hand rests on my velvet swathed knee, and I shiver as if the cloth did not exist. As if his musician's fingers, fine boned and strong, touched my bare skin. A touch both electric and sensual, like cold white wine drunk too much and too fast.

'You came all the way here. Why?'

He looks up at me, apologetic and burning all at once and I regret the sharp edge to my tone, the tinge of resentment that I've been without him, without even the consolation of his words or his voice so long. No matter that it was my own fault, my own wish that the break be clean and final.

'I tried, love. I'm sorry, I did. But I can't forget how it feels.' He sighs, shifts. 'I need to talk to you; I need to fuck you. I can't do this.'

I look out at the watery world, trying to ignore the impulse to stroke the droplets from his damp hair, to curl my fingers in the darkened strands.

'We broke the rules before. We broke them and didn't care,' he says, frowning when I turn to him.

'And part of the reason I left was to stop . . .'

'But it's hurting us. You told me it was an addiction, like any other kind. So why should we care about what the right thing is now anyway?

Why?' His voice rises, quavers in frustration and pain. Throwing my own demand to know back at me.

'Good question.'

I know he's still looking at me, stung by the indifference in my voice, but I avert my gaze. Find safety in watching water run in a haphazard trickle over some irregularity on the window frame. I'm still fighting the longing, fighting him. And I don't even know why.

'How can you be this cold?'

I shake my head. The rain falls in staccato needles, and a harp has joined the notes of the piano still pouring from the stereo speakers. I think I will break apart from longing and guilt.

I feel him move and I close my eyes. I know what will happen; it doesn't matter how cold or cruel I try to be. Yes. Yes, love, this is an addiction.

His hands turn my face to his, and my limbs betray me, taking me to the edge of the sofa, my arms going around him. His lips are rain cold and sweet; his clothing damp and chilled. But heat rises within him like a song, growing in tempo and sound.

He opens me. His hands search beneath my skirt, find the silken edges of my panties. He pulls them to my thighs, my knees. He slips them off one ankle and then another and, still kneeling, holds my feet together in his lap. Beneath his jacket and shirt his stomach is warm, vulnerable, and I rub my toes against that yielding, intimate space. He closes his eyes, cups my calves and massages them slowly.

It hurts to be shut out, even for a moment, and I whisper to him to look at me. I've already shut myself out for far too long. He smiles, obeys and bends to kiss my knees, trailing kisses down to the ticklish skin at the arch between knee and calf. Licking tiny, wet caresses up the undersides of my thighs as he pulls me forwards. As he takes my skirt off with practised ease. Tosses the cloth aside and turns to my belly. Water drops from his hair and piccolo kisses falling on the curve under my navel, the curve of my waist, up to the edges of my ribs.

This time I cannot help burying my hands in his hair. Arching under him and crying out as he makes love to me with these simple, soft kisses. Art without effort. But no, this isn't lovemaking; this is far beyond the simple, carnal weakness I was so afraid of once. This is worship and sacred song. It's as close to magic as I'll ever know.

His kisses are falling lower now, notes spiralling into a powerful melody. His tongue parts the folds of my sex, dancing over my clit, searching out the entrance to my pussy. Moving within me like a song of flame.

I lift his head and bring his lips to mine to kiss the fragrant, glistening moisture from his mouth. Tasting myself on him; taking myself back from him because all this while he's kept me safe while I ran. He runs his fingers up into my hair and down the back of my neck left bare by the short strands. He grasps the collar of my linen shirt and I hear the fabric tear, feel the touch of air as he eases the ruined garment down my arms. He kisses my shoulder as if to apologise for his impatient passion.

And I don't know how or why I should deserve this. Deserve him.

I lie naked on the sofa, watching him undress, and I think that he belongs here; his figure before the old-fashioned window, framed by bookcases and hand-carved chairs, that of a hero in a Regency romance. Body hard with muscle, hair long and tangled, the edges just brushing his chin. Serious and sensitive and melodramatic. All that I've ever wanted.

My fingers search between my legs to answer the need fuelled by the fantasy, by the longing. He is naked now too, but he stands still to watch, his full cock quivering as he takes in the sight of my spread legs, my fingers moving over the folds of my sex like a maestro's over ivory keys. He strokes himself, watching me, his gaze moving from my body to my face that I can feel is flushed with heat. In his eyes, I am Beauty.

'Don't stop,' he says as he comes to my side. He kneels and cups one breast in his hand.

The tip of his tongue brushes the nipple and the flesh between my legs thrums in answer. Another gentle lick and I'm melting in moans and sighs again. I tap my fingers faster against my swollen clit, fluttering movements driving the crescendo while his tongue plays accompaniment on my nipples, my belly, my parted lips.

He straddles my body, hand still moving along his cock, lips red from my kisses. Like a priest-king in some archaic ritual, waiting to offer his seed and his power to the priestess beneath him. Male and beautiful. He rubs the shaft of his cock along my sex and I'm ready to explode with sensation. Yet it's the thought of what he does – the way he does it, intense and deliberate – more than the action itself that puts me over the edge.

And while I'm still coming, still crying out with the satisfaction of orgasm, I feel him enter me. Feel the muscle of his cock sliding into my pussy, awakening even more feeling, taking away all pretence to decency. I forget the man and can think only of the delicious hardness driving into me.

But then he leans forwards and says my name, voice rough with arousal, and I remember the man. I remember why I have wanted him. All the days and nights of longing, the memories of forbidden trysting. All that I know now. The turmoil of emotion and thought joins the song, intensifying it, and helplessly I'm caught up in it while our bodies move.

The rain has become a torrent, beating itself wildly at the glass. Free and not free; trapped by bonds that cannot be seen. By duty. Obligation to fall. And so it falls with relentless passion.

We whisper to each other in short, breathless fragments. Things we should never say: desperate, filthy, loving. We leave bruises and bite marks. Something tangible to last, to prolong what is over too soon in a final burst of motion and inordinate cries. And then I clutch him to my sweat-soaked body, my breasts crushed by his weight, my legs folded tight about his. I press my face into his shoulder, breathing his scent. I'm surrounded by him; filled by him, inside and out. Safe.

The piano wafts sad and sweet over the subdued patter of rain. The music is always free and untethered by fear. The music will always win out over that which threatens to mute its voice. I promise myself that I won't run any more.

'How long do you have?' I ask, *pianissimo*.

'A few days,' he mumbles into the hollow of my neck. He lifts his regal, tousled head. 'Unless you let it be more.'

His tone is quiet, asking for nothing, but his eyes plead. I look away; I still can't give an answer. I know now that I'll do anything for him, but old habits and old fears are hard to let go of.

'Love . . .'

I shake my head, pulling his back down to my shoulder where I cannot see that gaze of longing. I'm giving in; it's only a matter of time. The music is weaving its spell and soon I will have no defences left. But not yet. He sighs and sinks into my arms, but he knows it too. The sounds of the piano and the rain run together, lull us to sleep. When we wake, he will make love to me again, and I will say yes.

A. D. R. Forte's short stories have appeared in numerous Wicked Words collections.

Rush Hour Cal Jago

I scanned the platform and took a step backwards, turning my head away from the sudden rush of air as the train roared into the station. The tube slowed to a standstill, a set of doors stopping directly in front of me. The carriage was almost empty. I picked up my briefcase and moved to the edge of the platform, pausing as a familiar sensation fluttered in my chest. The doors whooshed open and I strode along beside the train, passing two more sets of doors before I found the right one. Commuters were crammed into the tight space, squashed against the glass, tucked into the curves of the doorways, pressed up against one another. The perfect carriage. The perfect playground.

As the alarm sounded, signalling the imminent closure of the doors, I placed an impossibly high-heeled shoe on to the train, forcing my way into the heaving crowd. If there's one thing I've learned in almost ten years of commuting, it's that there's always room for one more – when that one more is me, obviously.

My last-minute entry meant that, as the train lurched into action, I was totally unprepared. The sudden movement flung me off-balance and straight into a fellow commuter. Not very dignified, but, as I looked up and saw my buffer, I realised that my being propelled into a stranger was something of a blessing. He was just right.

He was in his thirties, fair-haired with beautiful cheekbones. I smiled at him as I straightened myself up. 'I'm so sorry.'

He smiled back and looked a little embarrassed, the way people do on public transport when someone forces them into communication. 'No problem.'

I continued holding his gaze until his eyes flicked to my left and then down towards the floor. Except he wasn't looking at the floor.

'If I will insist on wearing silly shoes...' I continued lightly, shuffling a pointed toe in his direction.

He looked up and I noticed his face redden slightly.

A shy one. How sweet. How absolutely perfect.

I smiled again and then turned around so that my back was towards him, quickly scanning the area immediately surrounding me. A man who looked far too hot in far too many layers of clothing was fanning himself with a copy of *The Times* to my left. Beside me, on my right, a studenty-looking girl was staring into space tapping her fingers in time with whatever was playing on her iPod. Directly in front of me, with barely an inch of space between us, a middle-aged man was engrossed in a Sudoku puzzle, a phenomenon that had frankly passed me by. There are much more exciting things to do on train journeys than number-crunch. Believe me, I know. And, just for your information, before I'd crashed into him, my man had been reading a book – a John Grisham novel. Not very original, but strangely reassuring. Safe men read courtroom dramas, don't they? Psychos don't, I was sure.

As we raced into a tunnel, I very slowly and deliberately bent down, placing my briefcase on the floor. I moved from my waist, keeping my legs and knees absolutely straight – terrible for the back, I know, but, sometimes, needs must – and, as I busied myself with pointlessly positioning and repositioning my bag, I slung my weight onto my left hip.

Bingo. The weight shift had done it. My arse had swung slightly to the left and edged back a little, so, as I forced myself to lean lower still and made a show of hunting for something in my bag, I felt my buttocks brush against Grisham.

He cleared his throat and I felt him move. Whether he was trying to escape the physical contact or increase it, I couldn't tell, as I quickly straightened up. I stood in front of him, much closer than was necessary, even in spite of the fullness of the carriage. My behind was still touching him but the contact was barely perceptible. I felt his breath, hot and heavy, on the back of my neck. This looked promising.

We slowed down and jolted to a stop at the next station. Sudoku was on the move. Perfect. We all edged a little away from him, giving him space to manoeuvre. There was only one direction I was going to move in: backwards. The doors opened, we created a pathway for his exit, and he was gone. I stood pressed closely against Grisham, feeling the rise and fall of his chest against my shoulder blades and the nudging of his toes on the back of my heels. And there was no mistaking what else I could feel stirring against my arse.

I edged my right leg behind me and pressed the back of my thigh firmly against his hardening cock. I shifted my weight again, slowly grinding against his crotch, and felt a burst of hot breath blast against my neck. Game on.

I bent down again, lingering to scratch a non-existent itch on my shin, and swayed my hips from side to side, just enough movement to cause the friction I wanted. His breathing was shallow now and my knickers were distinctly damp. I straightened up and was surprised to suddenly feel his hand on my hip. His fingertips pressed into my skin, pulling me harder on to his cock. I continued to rock against him but was finding it difficult to remain discreet.

Determined though I was to keep control of myself, there was something I could not resist any longer. I eased my body away from his and felt his grip on my hip tighten. I reached back and gently rubbed the palm of my hand over the front of his trousers.

His fingers trailed along the curve of my hip, then grazed my arse, fluttering across the material of my tailored trousers. He began to caress more insistently, rubbing and squeezing my flesh, and then he drove his fingers between my legs in an effort to force my thighs apart. How easy it would have been to allow him to touch me there. But that wasn't part of the game. I twisted my lower body away from him.

I heard a low groan and quickly reached back, keeping the rest of my body at a safe distance. I closed my fingers around him, feeling his heat as I gripped his hardness, and I squeezed along his length, imagining the sight of him, his cock straining for release. I sensed the tension in every muscle in his body as he tried to keep his composure. He was struggling. He was not the kind of man who let strangers grope him on the train and he certainly wasn't the sort of man to make an exhibition of himself. And yet here we were. Even through the fabric of his trousers, I began to feel his cock pulse and twitch. He was going to come.

Perfect timing. As he tried desperately to hold on, we screeched into the next station. The doors opened and in a lightning moment I had released him, picked up my bag, barged past the student and exited the train.

I didn't look back, though I'd have liked to see the state I'd worked him into. I was curious as to whether the vision of his cock through his trousers was as impressive as the sensation of it in my hands. There was no doubt in my mind that it would have been. And I'd have liked to see the expression of sheer bloody disbelief on his face. It was an expression I'd seen so many times before – because sometimes I did look back – and it was one that sent an electric spasm between my thighs every time. How totally broken apart and lost they looked and how exhilarating to have been the cause of such undoing.

But, seconds later, my thoughts took a darker turn, as they often did. He would undoubtedly be pissed off. Would he really let me get away with it? Or would he follow me? Stalk me along the platform, shadow me through the exit barriers and track my movements on the streets above? Would he catch up with me, whisper angry words in my ear and demand to claim what had been promised? In short, would he be so desperate that he'd hunt me down and fuck me? And would I be so desperate for my own release that I would let him?

Needless to say, he didn't. He wouldn't. He would feel frustrated. Enraged, probably. He would think the word 'bitch', say it aloud even, a hiss of bitterness under his breath. But, ultimately, he wouldn't want to make a scene.

I always enjoyed the rush of those first couple

of minutes afterwards. Because no matter how many times I'd done it, or how confidently I strode, or how much absolute trust I had in my intuitive ability to choose my playmate for the journey, there was always, always, the very real possibility that I could fuck it all up. There was always a chance that I'd pick the wrong man.

The cacophony of voices, traffic and general city noise brought some clarity to my frenzied mind as I exited the underground and made my way along the busy street above. But, still, my body was buzzing as I walked the familiar route to work.

There had been countless Grishams. My first hit was accidental, so I suppose it doesn't really count as a hit, but that was what started it all off, so I feel I should mention it. I had left work later than usual and was in a panic because I was sure I was going to miss my train, which in turn would have led me to be late for a dinner date with my then boyfriend. I'd sprinted down the platform, my heart sinking as I saw that the train was packed. A seat was out of the question, but would there be standing room for one more? Well, of course there was, but only just. It was the tightest of squeezes. I forced my way into a vestibule area at the back of the train just as the guard blew his whistle and the door was slammed shut behind me. There were so many of us in that tiny area, all standing in far closer proximity than we would have in any other circumstance. As the train rumbled along we all rocked together, bumping into one another a little, stumbling slightly and reaching out instinctively to keep our balance. I was pressed against a businessman: tall, broad, fortyish. We stood facing each other, my cheek almost touching his shoulder. We were a few minutes into the journey when I finally realised exactly where my hand had ended up when I'd tried to grab something to prevent toppling over. I felt myself blush but, as I went to remove my hand, the man took hold of my wrist, keeping me in position. All things considered, I guess he was a bit of a pervert. But, judging by the immediate drenching of my underwear, I guess I was too.

Trains had always, in my mind, been a great location for crotch watching. One of my favourite commuting pastimes up until that point had been sitting staring – discreetly, of course – at all the sights that met my eyeline You know how it is when sometimes you just want something? Well, Pervy Businessman made me realise just how easy it was to get it.

My first deliberate hit was just a few days after my liaison with Pervy. I hadn't managed to get it out of my head: his sheer audacity making me touch him like that in a crowded carriage. More than that, though, I couldn't get over how much it had turned me on. So one morning I found myself standing near the luggage hold during rush hour. A man was standing opposite me, quiet, unassuming. He looked respectable. Safe. Just as we arrived at the final station stop, we both gathered our belongings ready to move off the train. I had a quick look over my shoulder to check that no one was immediately behind us, then I took a deep breath, reached out and touched him. He turned to me sharply and opened his mouth as though to speak but he remained silent. I rubbed just a little and then squeezed his cock firmly, and then I was gone, speeding along the platform, heart thumping wildly and with a huge grin on my face. It had lasted no more than a few seconds but I couldn't believe I had done it or that I'd got away with it. And I knew then that I was addicted.

You're probably thinking that the leaving part is cruel, and I suppose, if I'm honest, it is. But I enjoy the power of it. Not that it always ends that way. Sometimes they get to come. Unfortunately for Grisham, he was simply a victim of timing. Early-morning meetings really could play havoc with a girl's social life.

My office building was one of those ultra-modern marvels – all open-plan work areas and glass-walled meeting rooms. It was a hive of creativity, containing everything required to produce some of the biggest magazine titles in the country. As the managing editor of the glossy women's monthly, I had an office in the middle of the main editorial area, but that wasn't where I headed straightaway.

I swiped my security pass in the main reception area, took the lift to the third floor and ignored the coffee cart, which was usually my first port of call. I headed straight to the staff toilets, swung a cubicle door open with far more force than I had intended, then locked it behind me and stood with my back to it. I slid one hand down inside the front of my trousers and then hooked a couple of fingers under the cloth of my underwear. I smiled with relief as my fingers began their exploration. There were certainly worse ways to start a Monday morning.

'Kate?' It was Natalie, my PA. 'Is that you?'

For fuck's sake! My hand froze, hovering inside my knickers. I leaned my head back against the door and closed my eyes.

'Kate?'

'Yep,' I said as cheerily as I could. 'It's me.'

'Thought so. Look, I thought I'd better warn you: I've just done the latest cover report and we seem to have forty grand unaccounted for.'

'Unaccounted for?' I sighed and repositioned my clothing, then flushed the loo. Well, thousands of pounds going missing does tend to quash one's ardour – as does having your PA standing with her ear almost up against the door when you're trying to come. I emerged from the cubicle.

'Morning,' Natalie beamed and then quickly became serious again. 'Yes, as in "missing". As in "we've clearly spent it but fuck knows how, where or why".'

I sighed again as I squirted soap onto my hands. It smelled of peaches. How very 80s.

'Also ...' I looked at her warily and she smiled apologetically. 'Lindsay Sharman is kicking up a stink about her contract. As in she says we're in breach of it.'

I raised my eyebrows in alarm.

'Personally,' Natalie said conspiratorially, 'I think she's after a bit more money because her column's just won an award. I've dug her contract out and left it on your desk.'

'Thanks. In the meantime, send her some flowers and invite her out for lunch, will you? Sometime next week. I'm sure we can't be in the wrong with this, but I want to keep hold of her.'

I shook my hands over the basin and turned around to find Natalie in front of me holding out a paper towel. 'And also ...' she began.

'Are you serious?'

''Fraid so.'

I snatched the towel from her and began to dab at my hands.

'Have you seen the papers this morning?' she asked.

I faltered. 'No. I was working on the train,' I lied.

'Working? On the tube as well?' She pulled a face. 'I don't know how you can. I hate the tube – why don't you just let me arrange for a car to pick you up in the mornings? Much more civilised.'

'As I've told you before, I'm doing my bit for the environment,' I said doing my best not to look shifty.

'Well, I think you're mad. Anyway, the papers. Maya Singleton has been outed in all the tabloids. There are photos of her and her girlfriend looking all lovey-dovey, which doesn't in any way reflect the content of our interview with her.'

I groaned. Maya Singleton was the hottest British property in Hollywood and we had bagged an exclusive with her a few weeks before.

'So, basically, that's October's cover and main interview feature shot to shit,' Natalie concluded. 'And, if you're wondering why I've accosted you in the loo, it's because Alex is waiting for you in your office so I thought I'd better prepare you.'

As if I didn't have enough to deal with without the publishing director pouncing on me as soon as I get through the door.

I smiled weakly. 'Thanks, Nat. And, when you've got a minute, would you mind . . .'

'There's a latte on your desk.'

Sometimes, I thank God for Natalie.

Miraculously, the day actually panned out far more positively than the frantic exchange in the loo had led me to expect. A bit of creative thinking and a whole lot of charm meant that, by the time I left the office at 9 p.m., all crises had been pretty much averted.

I slumped, exhausted, into a window seat and

willed the train to go faster. The day had presented one major challenge after another and I
was looking forward to a soak in the bath and a
glass or three of Shiraz. That didn't, however, stop
somebody from catching my eye: a boot-shod
woman sitting across the aisle. She was very
attractive, petite but curvy with dark hair and
dark eyes. A small smile played at the corners of
her mouth, which, together with her smart
though somewhat rumpled appearance, gave her
a just-shagged look, which I found rather appealing. There were a number of factors working
against me here, of course. First, I barely had the
strength to blink. Secondly, we were both sitting
down. In my experience, standing was much better – easier access, easier to make any physical
contact look accidental, easier to move position
and conceal any sauciness, and easier to escape
should a kerfuffle ensue. The final obstacle was,
of course, that she was a woman.

It's not that I didn't want to play with women
– I most definitely did and, on occasion, I had. It's
just that they were tricky. If choosing a male
playmate was a risky business, picking a woman
was a million times more so. Fundamentally, the
crux of the matter was this: no man had ever
turned me down. OK, some were up for more
than others, some played for a little while, then
left rather hastily, some looked quite appalled
with themselves – and probably with me too. But
not one of them had told me 'no' or pushed me

away. Are they just not fussed? Will they take anything going? Perhaps they simply have less to lose and, if some woman wants to grab their dick on their way to work, yippee. Women, I like to think, are far more complex creatures. Anyway, whether my Great Gender Theory was right or not, I remain convinced that a woman is far more likely to reject me so I'm always cautious.

That said, one of my favourite hits of all time was a woman. I had known I wanted her as soon as I had spotted her on the platform but I'd deliberated for ages because she looked so straight. Also, we were waiting for an overground train; the first stop wasn't for half an hour, so, if I made a move and she didn't want to play, I wouldn't be able to escape. But we entered the same coach and both stood at the end of the carriage, so I steeled myself and approached her. I had my hand up her skirt in a matter of seconds and had never felt a woman so wet. I buried my fingers deep inside her and fucked her deliciously slowly as we sped through the Thames Valley, her eyes locked with mine all the time as she stared in surprise while her muscles contracted around me. So determined was I to make her come that I flew past my stop and ended up alighting at Slough. Sometimes, alighting at Slough is worth it.

I turned away from the Booted One. Attracted to her though I was, it just wasn't going to happen. Sometimes, the desire to sleep is just too great.

* * *

The remainder of the week past quickly: more meetings, more financial headaches and plenty more train journeys to keep me occupied. Although, I have to confess, I had been very well behaved during my travels since Grisham – until the morning I found myself standing next to Issey Miyake on the tube. Well, a man wearing his aftershave, anyway.

He had caught my eye and smiled and I'd smiled back. He was good-looking and impeccably dressed. His suit looked expensive, though he stood in his shirtsleeves with his jacket slung casually over his shoulder. I felt drawn to him and found myself pressed against him in no time. I was going to enjoy this.

'I've seen you before,' he said suddenly, his mouth close to my ear.

I felt momentarily unsettled, unaccustomed to having to make conversation in such circumstances, but his voice was warm and my unease quickly dissipated. A voyeur who liked what he saw and has waited patiently for his turn – I liked that.

'Really?' I asked, in my lightest, most flirtatious voice. 'And what did you see?' I pushed out my bottom slightly so that it nudged at his crotch.

'You,' he said, gently caressing the back of my thigh.

I smiled. 'Yes?' I reached back to touch him, but, as I did so, found my wrist caught in his hand.

'Being a prick-tease,' he continued, tightening his grip on my wrist.

I gasped in surprise as he continued to squeeze my flesh. Without thinking, I tried to turn and flung my other arm back in an attempt to free myself, a move he was obviously anticipating because he immediately ensnared that wrist too.

A quick risk assessment told me that the situation was obviously not good: I had been grabbed by a stranger with a somewhat threatening demeanour and was unsure how I was going to escape. My heart rate quickened as fear combined with something just as potent; I felt inexplicably weak-kneed with lust and I was appalled at myself. I continued to twist a little in an attempt to break free but he held me firm.

Perhaps, I thought suddenly, this had been the point of the game all along: to find a player as equally skilled as I was. In which case, surely I had to step up now. To call out for help or catch someone's eye so that they rushed to my aid or even to struggle until he released me would all mean the end of the game. And, although people would take my side and he could end up in a whole heap of trouble, ultimately, I couldn't help thinking that I would have lost. And I was a sore loser. Something told me he realised that. Something also told me he wasn't intent on making trouble. He was just out to play. At least, I hoped so.

When we arrived at the next station, I was not

surprised to be shoved forward. We made our way through the throng of commuters on the platform, he walking slightly behind me so he could keep me close without anyone being able to see how he was holding me. I assumed we were heading for the exit but, as I followed the crowd in that direction, he steered me another way. We ducked under a chain sporting a NO ENTRY sign and headed down a steep stairwell. It was difficult keeping my footing with my hands pulled behind me, but, for some reason, I trusted him not to let me fall. I looked around. There was nothing there, just a small area with a barred gate leading to a narrow underground corridor.

He positioned me in front of the gate and stood behind me, retaining his one-handed grip on me. Then I felt movement and heard the rustle of clothing and panicked momentarily – this was all happening too fast. But within seconds his grip on my wrists slackened and I felt the coolness of silk snaking its way across my skin. He fastened his tie securely around both my wrists. It wasn't tight enough to hurt, but it was firm enough to immobilise me.

'Just so we're clear,' he said, '*I'm* playing with *you* now, not the other way around.'

I felt my face flush and my skin prickle as I considered the notion of simply being his toy, passive and vulnerable. The thought was not one that appealed. I couldn't suppress a sigh as I contemplated the fact that I thought I'd given up unsatisfactory sex years ago. What was the point in this?

His hands delicately traced their way across the small of my back and over my hips before coming together to meet on the swell of my buttocks. Then they skimmed downwards until they came to rest on the back of my thighs. He stroked across the fabric of my skirt and then ventured lower. I felt his fingers glide across my stockinged legs as he dived under my skirt, his touch gentle but insistent. I frowned, hating the fact that he was touching me while I couldn't touch him and knowing that there was nothing I could do about it. My skirt hitched as his hand pushed higher, locating the very tops of my stockings. He lingered there, rubbing his fingertips across the coarseness of the lace trim. An unmistakable sigh escaped from his lips as he touched the bare skin of my thighs. Perhaps I had overestimated his control. A smile twitched at the corners of my mouth. This would be easier than I had expected.

'You like that?' I teased and I leaned back a little so that my bound hands just about made contact with his crotch.

He moved back at once. 'Do you like this?' he asked and tugged the tie, making my upper body jerk backwards.

I cried out in surprise and felt ashamed of myself for reacting so pitifully. But then the silk fell away from my wrists and I turned to face him, smiling triumphantly. I had known that he wouldn't be able to hold out on me for long.

He flashed a broad smile, which caught me off-guard, and the next thing I knew he'd grasped my hands again and was tying them in front of me.

'You can't be trusted, I see,' he said, raising my hands slightly so that my arms were outstretched. He stepped forward, turning my body as he moved so that I was facing the gate again, and then he reached forward and deftly fastened the end of the tie to the rails. I went to speak – to object – but then thought better of it. The last thing I wanted was for him to think he had ruffled me. So I stood with my head resting on my hands against the railings, determined not to give anything away.

His hand moved up my legs and then hovered between my thighs. Despite my good intentions to stay in control, I was aroused and, when his fingers at last made contact with the place that yearned for it most, it took an unbelievable amount of effort to remain silent. I bit down on my lip as his fingers began to tease; back and forth they slid across the soft cotton, and then I felt cool air rush across my skin as my knickers were eased down and pooled at my feet. I took a deep breath. This hadn't been what I'd intended when I'd set off for work but I couldn't deny that I was excited.

'You like that?' he asked.

I shrugged, determined not to reveal the unexpected effect he was having on me.

He chuckled. 'You don't want to answer me?'

I cleared my throat and then shook my head.

The shock of his flattened palm making contact with my bare arse threw me off-balance and I momentarily swung a little on the short length of tie that was slackly holding me to the rail. I managed to steady myself quickly but the turn of events had taken me completely by surprise. Apart from anything else, I was shocked by his confidence, his boldness.

A second smack followed, and then another. He barely paused between smacks and I shut my eyes tight, my ears ringing with the sounds of skin-to-skin contact. I gasped with the suddenness each time – the sound, the force, the way it made my body jolt – and I determined to focus on the pain that was spreading across my arse. Well, not so much pain as heat. And, between my legs, fire raged.

I felt him move behind me, then his hands gently held my bottom. His breath cooled my burning skin and my body froze as I stood exposed. Seconds later, his tongue pressed against my tender flesh, tracing along the marks I imagined he must have left on my body. The sensation was excruciatingly sublime as the wetness from his mouth sent chills through my hot skin. My head swirled. Part of my brain still willed me not to give in but my body hummed and all I could think about was how much I wanted to come. I needed to. I hadn't been this desperate for months. But I just couldn't let myself.

'Stop it,' I whispered, breathless. I closed my eyes. 'You have to stop.'

His hands remained on my arse and when he spoke, his lips brushed against my sensitive flesh. 'You want me to stop?' he asked, and then the tip of his tongue zigzagged down my lower back before coming to a stop at the cleft between my buttocks.

I held my breath.

'Are you sure you want me to stop?'

I murmured an indecipherable sound and his tongue returned to my body, gliding its wetness along my centre, making me shiver. Before I knew what I was doing I had instinctively leaned further forward, exposing myself to him completely. He didn't waste a second. He held my thighs wider apart and then pushed his face between them. I moaned as his tongue lapped at my entrance and bent lower allowing him to tickle my clit with the softest motions. I gripped the railings as my thighs began to tremble and he pressed his whole mouth against me, stimulating me with his chin, nose, mouth, everything. I squirmed against him as my orgasm built. And then, nothing, his presence between my legs, gone.

'No,' I whispered, turning around to look at

him over my shoulder. He was standing upright now, grinning at me.

'I decided you were right,' he said. 'You know, when you said about stopping.'

I stared at him in amazement. The muscles in my arms, I now realised, were burning having been held up for so long, and my arse was sore from the spanking. But my pussy was pounding. 'Is this payback?' I asked at last.

'I thought you needed teaching a lesson,' he said, stepping closer. 'How not to be a bad girl to men on trains.' He smiled. 'But you obviously can't take it . . .'

'Of course I can take it,' I said indignantly. Although, of course, I couldn't.

'Really?' He stood directly behind me and reached for my clit. I gasped despite myself and writhed against his hand as he teased and rubbed for a few brief moments before stopping again.

'Please,' I said in frustration.

'Please what?' He stood so closely to me that I could feel his breath on my skin. And for the first time, I felt his rock-hard cock straining against my leg.

I bit down on my lip. God, I was desperate.

'Hmm?' He dipped a finger inside me, coating it with my wetness, and groaned as he began to slowly finger-fuck me. 'Please what?' My muscles tightened around him drawing him deeper. 'If your pussy is anything to go by,' he said slowly, 'I'd say you were losing your resolve.'

I couldn't help but smile then. 'And you're not?' I asked as another finger pushed deep inside me. 'Because something tells me this wasn't meant to happen.' I pushed my leg back slightly, nudging his hardness. 'I think you brought me down here to tease me a bit and then leave me wanting. But you haven't left,' I said feeling suddenly bold. He began to thrust his fingers harder. 'Oh.' I tried to concentrate on what I was saying. 'And you haven't left,' I said, bucking slightly to meet his thrust, 'because you want to fuck me.'

'I want to fuck you?' He withdrew my fingers and I panicked for a moment until I felt his fingers circling my clit.

I closed my eyes. I was so close but, now I'd said it, I wanted it so badly. 'Yes,' I hissed.

'Is that what you think?'

'Mmm.' I was starting to feel light-headed.

'And is that what you want?' I heard his zip ease down.

'Yes,' I whispered. 'God, please, fuck me.'

His whole length was inside me in an instant. He grabbed my left hip with one hand as he drove into me with long, smooth strokes and his other hand returned to my clit. My bound hands gripped the rail until the knuckles faded to white and I pushed myself back forcefully against him, meeting every one of his powerful thrusts. I couldn't remember the last time I had felt so positively taken. He slammed into me harder, all the while rubbing and pinching my clit until it felt ready to burst. I could feel his muscles quivering and his breathing quickened as he began to thrust more rapidly. Then he reached forward and covered my hand with his, an action that, along with his fingers on my clit and his hardness inside me, pushed me over the edge. I came hard, my legs suddenly weak, my wrists shaking against the silk that held me in place; and, shortly afterwards, he climaxed too, burying himself deeper inside me and shouting out close to my ear.

I leaned heavily against the gate and closed my eyes as I waited for my breathing to steady. I could hear him adjusting his clothes and smelled a waft of his scent as he moved closer to me. My wrists began to tingle and I realised that they had been untied. I slowly straightened up and let my arms drop heavily to my sides. They ached and I stretched while clenching and unclenching my fingers in an attempt to loosen them up.

'They've gone a bit numb,' I said, but I knew as I said the words that they were unnecessary. And sure enough, when I turned around, he had gone.

Cal Jago's short stories have appeared in numerous Wicked Words collections.

Number 1 Candy Wong

There was a sharp vegetable tang to the room: dirt-caked boots, she thought, and damp clothes crushed to the bottom of nylon kit-bags and left to fester for another week. It was always the same, the smell, and yet for ever strange to her, unpleasant and yet attractive in some way she couldn't put her finger on, arousing something primal in her. Kneeling forwards, she tied her laces with two brisk tugs, then clutched her stick across her chest and left the room.

The cold spanked her across the face, but the contrast with the overheated changing room was invigorating. She inhaled deeply and set off for the patch of green behind the line of trees to the right of the building. On the field she could see a few figures already limbering up, smudges of black against the blank white sky.

She was almost level with the shed when the girls appeared at her shoulders, like dark angels. One of them – she wasn't sure if it was pin-thin Julie with her lank tawny hair or the more rounded Jane with her frizzy halo of strawberry-blonde curls – shot out an elbow that caught her in the ribs and made her yell out.

'Oi! Goalie,' quipped Jane with a sardonic smile. 'Seen lover boy yet? He in there?'

Tamara hazarded a glance at the shed. The door swung open on its hinges but no one was inside among the massed ranks of gardening tools and little pots of seedlings.

But Jane had barely paused for a reply before adding, 'Oh no, you won't have, will you? He'll be out there already, waiting for you.' She turned to Julie triumphantly, and the pair snickered conspiratorially.

Tamara chewed her lip and looked back towards the playing field. She hoped her college-mate was wrong, but feared that too. His presence embarrassed her, and more so the longer it went on, but if he wasn't there today then something would have changed in some obscure way that she wouldn't be able to fathom because she didn't know why he was there to begin with, and why he looked at her the way he did.

At first she'd tried to tell herself that it wasn't her, that he was watching all of them. But then the others − and not just spite-filled Jane and Julie − had started to make remarks, and she'd had to admit to herself that she was why he came, drove his spade hard into the earth and folded his arm over the handle as he followed her about the pitch with his small black eyes.

They were almost at the field now and she could hear the other girls tittering behind her as they made him out at the other end of the field, immobile, taking deep drags on a cigarette and blowing smoke out into the freezing air.

'What would dear old Trissy say,' called Julie, 'if he knew about your secret admirer? Your bit of rough? He wouldn't be too thrilled about it, I'm sure.'

Tamara ignored the tacit threat; she'd long since concluded that to rise to Jane and Julie would only encourage them, let them think they had some kind of hold over her. Which they didn't. She didn't give a stuff what they said to her or about her. Or what they said to other people, least of all Tristan. She reached the half-way line and began to bend and stretch.

Gradually the remaining players filtered on to the pitch and Mrs Wass blew her whistle for the two centres to bully off. There followed an hour of fairly uninspired play, with lots of dribbling up and down the field by the wings but few shots at either end. Tamara far preferred the cut and thrust of real games to these practice sessions, which lacked any feeling of aggression or risk, especially as the last game of the campaign had been played. This training session had a pointless, empty feeling to it. *A bit like Tristan*, she thought, and giggled quietly at her own cruelty.

Her position in the team meant that, when she wasn't required to actively defend her goal, there really wasn't much for her to do, and that in turn increased her self-consciousness. Throughout the game she was aware of the man at the limits of her vision, always there, like a fault on her retina, and she was haunted by the danger of inadvertently meeting his gaze. So she was glad whenever she did see a little action, when she got the chance to hurl her body at oncoming balls, savouring the feel of the cold mud as it slicked across her knees and thighs.

Afterwards, as she peeled off her kit in the changing room with its misted-up windows, its radiators steaming with sweaty socks and its almost cloacal smell, she found herself thinking about him, really thinking, for the first time. She didn't know what he looked like, not from close up, or even how old he was, not to mention what was going through his mind as he watched her leap and dive, brandishing her stick like some kind of weapon. His scrutiny had affected her though. She felt dizzy, thickened in the throat as if she had been embarrassed in front of her fellow players. She was warm and tingling in places that she really ought not to be, especially on such a chilly day.

Pulling her sports bra up over her head, enjoying the brief chafe of rough cotton against her nipples, she became aware that stick-insect Julie, with her slightly bulging, reptilian eyes and her small tight mean mouth, was staring at her across the room. They'd been mates once, the three of them, and then, out of the blue, the other two had turned on her. She'd never understood why. Now, as she saw how Julie's gaze flickered over her planes and curves, lingering for one barely perceptible moment on her breasts with their mocha areolae, she thought she knew why. The gardener wasn't the only one who thought Tamara had a beautiful body. Well, let them admire her. She arched her body as she reached into her locker for the shampoo, aware of how her breasts would rise and separate, her tummy become taut, perhaps even bring a little of her bush into view above the waistband of her shorts. She pretended to be distracted by some minuscule piece of grit on her chest and swept it away, careful to brush her fingers over the stiffened flesh of her left breast, which jiggled in just the way she wanted.

She glanced at Julie as she made her way to the showers. Her erstwhile friend was red in the face, trying to keep a towel around her own nudity, which wasn't as bad as her clumsy attempts at modesty suggested. She was thin, sure, and her ribs were painfully visible, but she had perky boobs with generous, rude pink nipples and a good curve to her hips. Her bum was firm and round. Tamara almost laughed out loud. Being leched over on a hockey pitch seemed to be all she needed to get her in a froth to the extent that she could begin having fantasies about her teammates.

In the shower, camouflaged by steam, she soaped her breasts for a long time, paying more attention than was necessary to the nipples, which felt so hard under her fingers that she thought they would never again turn soft. But as much as she wanted to she couldn't bring herself to rub her pussy. Not yet. Not when so many things about her body, about sex, about Tristan, were still so uncertain. She noticed other girls spending inordinate amounts of time with loofahs or flannels or bare fingers, bent over, mashing them against the soft flesh of their pussies. She heard the squishing of thick lather and the low sighs barely audible above the hissing showerheads. She wished for some of their daring. As she stepped from the shower she smelt the unmistakeable aroma of female sex and wondered why it was that, no matter how much she dabbed the towel against her sex, she could not get it dry.

Back home, alone in the house, she tried to finish some coursework as she waited for Tristan to arrive. But her thoughts kept returning to the figure lurking at the end of the hockey pitch, to that face barely visible beneath the hood of his ample jacket, pulled up against the wind and rain, to those eyes trained on her. When the doorbell rang, she started as if from a trance.

'Hi Tam,' said Tristan, blustering in in his tracksuit.

She returned his kiss briefly, then led him into the kitchen, where a pot of pasta and sauce spat and bubbled on the hob. After ladling some into two large white bowls, she sprinkled them with grated Parmesan from a packet and set them down on the breakfast bar, at which Tristan was by now seated.

She barely spoke, mechanically taking in forkfuls of pasta and letting his talk of student-union politics and rowing victories wash over her. She looked at his smooth face, at his skin, unblemished, almost supernaturally clean, at his ash-blond hair and thought again of those words of her mother – 'If I were twenty years younger, God almighty . . .' The look on her face as she had said it – Tamara would never forget that. Tristan was, by anyone's standards, the university catch. The face of an angel with the physique of a Greek god. The golden boy. Who could resist?

He needed to be gone by seven, he told her as he rejected the brownie she offered him. That gave them an hour to kill. His perfect white teeth flashed at her as he grinned. She let the dishes clatter into the sink, wiped her hands on some kitchen roll and followed him into her bedroom.

He was bare-chested on the bed before she had even crossed the threshold, hands behind his head, a knowing smile on his lips. She stopped, looked at his hairless chest, at his flat brown stomach with its encroaching mesh of curls the colour of burned sugar. Lowering herself on to the bed, she placed her hand on his belly and brought her face down to him, inhaling the mint and tea-tree aromas of his deodorant. He encircled her upper arm with his hand, quite tightly, and pulled her up towards him, his lips seeking hers.

'I'm still hungry,' he said when she finally pulled her head away.

'Tris,' she began. Already she hated the whiney tone in her voice.

'Oh, Christ, Tam.' His chest rose and fell heavily. 'Not a-bloody-gain.'

'I'm just not sure –'

'Not sure I'm ready.' His voice rose a few octaves in imitation of hers.

'Tris, please. Just –'

He sat up, threw his shoulders back and looked at her with those baby-blue eyes of his, a look that said, 'They all want me, I could have any girl I want, and you dare to refuse me. Who the hell do you think you are?'

'OK,' she conceded, tearing her gaze away from his, bending forward to undo her shoes.

At once he was upon her, dragging her back on to the bed by her shoulders, then rolling her over and pushing her skirt up over her thighs. All the while his mouth was on hers, his tongue probing her. She struggled to breathe, felt suffocated. She felt his hands tugging at her knickers, felt the give of the elastic over her buttocks as they were yanked down. Then he sat up, and she watched appalled as he slipped his tracksuit bottoms down over his hips, revealing a flawless cock that looked polished as a pebble, scrubbed and pink as a mollusc emerged from its shell. A clean velvety

cock that demanded to be held and to be wor-
shipped. He was holding it in his hand, as if
proffering it to her. She took it gently in her fist
and watched as its little gummy eye wept a clear
tear for her. She leant forwards, hesitantly, and
flicked it away with her tongue. It tasted salty
and warm, like jellied sea water. Tristan's lips
pulled back from his teeth and a hiss of satisfaction escaped between them. His face was darken-
ing. She watched, amazed by the simple power
she was wielding over him, as the tip of his cock
pulsed and reddened. He was trying to thrust
against her grip, to roll his foreskin back under
her fingers, but she wasn't moving against his
motion.

'Please,' he said.

She dipped her hand beneath his balls and ran
a fingernail along along the seam of his sac. He
trembled, threatening to fall against her. Another
tear of pre-come dripped across her wrist. She
opened her mouth and placed the throbbing bulb
of his cock beneath her lips, without touching
him. She breathed hot air over him, allowed her
saliva to drizzle his head. He sounded as if he
might start crying. But something felt wrong.

She released him and he fell back, his eyes
open and shocked. 'What?' he managed.

She couldn't put it into words. But it was something to do with the way that it was suddenly
more about the actual act than any intimacy
between them. She felt that she could have been

anyone and he would have been happy. He didn't pay her any heed, not like the gardener. She was invisible to Tristan; she was something hot and wet to deposit in when he wanted to. Well, not while she was in control of things.

She moved back over the bed, away from him, pulling her skirt down. 'I can't, Tris.'

He stared at her, then before she could say a word packed himself away, hastily, leaving his shirt untucked, and pulled on his tracksuit top. 'I've fucking had it with you, you frigid cow,' he shouted on his way out of the room.

She lay on the bed and listened to doors slamming as he made his way through the house and back out on to the street. Then she undressed fully, retrieved a pot of yogurt from the fridge and went to run a bath.

As the sweet scent of geranium oil permeated the air, she looked at herself in the mirror. Like Tristan, she had a kind of physical perfection that aroused lust in many, envy in some, not least Jane and Julie. Not that she cared about that. Who wanted to hang out with bitches like that anyway? She was glad to be rid of them. But something was bothering her and, as she looked at her long lean limbs and symmetrical curves, she realised what it was: no matter what everybody else said about him, not matter how much even her own mother wantonly lusted after him, she just couldn't find Tristan sexy. Did that mean there was something wrong with her?

For months now, ever since they started seeing each other, he'd been coming around after working out at the gym, rubbing her breasts, putting his hands further and further up her skirt. It didn't matter how often she'd protested, or what form that protest took – I'm only seventeen; I've got my period; my housemates are going to be home any minute – he was determined to get her between the sheets. She'd thought it was fear; now she realised his basic lack of respect for her – his reducing of her to a pair of tits and a tight pussy – revolted her.

Or was it sex itself that revolted her? Still looking at herself in the full-length mirror, she sank to the tiled floor. She pulled her long auburn hair back with one hand and studied her face. Perhaps she was just one of those non-physical people you heard about sometimes. People who just don't have any interest in sex, who can go a whole lifetime without. She opened her legs and stared between them in the mirror. Her lips, surrounded by downy fronds of copper-coloured hair, gaped a little, allowing her to see into the nest of pinks and reds. It was darker than she had imagined, meatier, more swollen. She thought of butcher's shop windows, of slabs of steak, but the image didn't disturb her. She licked her fingers and brought them to her pussy. She'd never even masturbated before. Did that mean she was asexual? Did all the other first-year girls wank?

She glanced down again. She was wet. She

moved her fingers and began to explore her folds and creases, the delicate petals of herself. She closed her eyes. This was *good*. This was better than good. She reached for the towel beside her, slid it beneath her and lay back, spilling the yogurt as she did so. Fuck it, she thought. To her left she could hear water coursing from the taps and wondered vaguely if she should get up and turn them off before the bath overflowed, but before she could decide a jag of pleasure ripped through her loins. It was as if she'd touched some button. That must be my clit, then, she thought. She gasped, laughed, swore. Her free hand lashed out and smeared the slick of yogurt. She brought it back to its twin and slathered the cool, creamy stuff all over her hot pussy. Her fingers squelched and sucked inside her as she delved for a rare sensation that stayed tantalisingly out of reach. Everything she was seemed focused now on the hole at her core. She didn't recognise the creature in the mirror, hair plastered to her forehead, hands jammed between her legs, her breasts quivering as she hit a rhythm that she knew would bring her the climax she desired. Stars danced inside her.

'Tamara, are you in?' she heard from the hallway, and she stifled a moan of frustration, jumped up and climbed into the bath, submerging herself completely.

* * *

She rose in the dark, dressed in silence and left the house. She hadn't worked out how she was going to get there, but when she saw Dave's bike leaning against the fence she figured he wouldn't notice if it went missing for an hour or two.

She rode through the streets, through the orange pools of light cast by the streetlamps, looking up at the dark windows she passed, wondering what people were dreaming of behind their closed curtains, or what they were doing to each other across the beds, up against the walls, on the stairs ... She travelled slowly; she wasn't in a hurry. She'd dressed in her hockey shorts – they were to hand – and the night air was icy on her bare legs. She felt more alive than ever before.

The gate was locked, as she had known it would be, but the wall was easy to scale for someone as athletic as her. She paused as she hit the ground, looked around her at the strangeness of the deserted park laid out beneath the moon. It could just have been that she was spaced out from not sleeping and from the shock of the glacial air in her lungs as she pedalled, but she didn't think so. To see this public space, usually so full of activity – not just hockey players, but dog-walkers, joggers, gangs of schoolboys sneaking a cigarette in the lunch break, little old men napping on benches – devoid of all life and movement was bizarre. It was like entering an alien territory where none of the familiar rules applied.

She followed the main path towards the house, then continued to the right when it forked. The shed lay a few steps away, side on to the house and the door to the changing room. She hesitated. Part of her wanted to go into the changing room, to inhale its rich, earthy odours of sweat and mud and rot, of old forgotten things. But she was pretty sure that would be locked too. The shed, on the other hand, she could see from where she stood that the door to that was ajar, and that a faint light emanated from within. She stepped up and grasped the handle, her breath caught in her throat.

He was working by the light of a storm lamp, a cigarette crumbling to ash in an ashtray beside him. He was rapt in his work, easing his sturdy fingers down into the soil and moving them carefully until he had loosened the root system and could pull the seedling out. Beside him on the wooden workbench were a row of larger pots to hold the burgeoning plants.

He hadn't heard her pull the door open, and she was able to watch him a while. She could see his face clearly now, side on at least, and the first thought that came to her was that he was hairy, very hairy. He didn't have a beard, but his stubble was advanced, his eyebrows thick and unruly, and she could even make out a few hairs sprouting along the line of his cheekbone. His hair, now that it wasn't hidden by a hood, appeared bushy and tangled, with sprinklings of grey. His eyes were small, intent, inspecting every plant as he transferred it over to its new home. He seemed to stroke them as he did so, give them an encouraging or reassuring little rub with his fingertips.

She looked him up and down, noted that he was shorter than she had realised, probably a little shorter than herself, with a slight paunch. His clothes, corduroy trousers and a brown jumper, were worn and ill-fitting. But it was his hands to which her eyes kept returning, those weathered extremities with their mud-encrusted nails, their surfaces lined as road maps. It was as if dirt had worked its way into every pore and crevice, year on year, until it had become a part of his very being. Those hands, she thought, were this man's life. His contact with the universe. She imagined them on her, rough and greedy, leaving grubby fingerprints on her clean innocent breasts.

He had stopped now, and stood expressionless, looking down at his workbench. He seemed lost in a reverie, and suddenly she felt like an intruder. She had no right to be watching him like this. At least when he watched her, both parties knew about it, and all the other players too. This was something else.

She walked away, out past the house and the door to the changing room towards the pitch. She didn't know what time it was, but thought that the sky seemed a little paler now than when she had arrived. She hadn't got far when she heard a noise behind her, and when she looked over her shoulder she saw that the shed door was closed. So he *had* been aware of her, she thought, and now he was shutting her out. That was fair enough. She had been spying on him and he'd been too polite or too shy to tell her to go away. He was obviously a loner, wasn't good at dealing with things like that. But she'd overstepped the boundaries.

Then she heard the footsteps behind her on the path and she realised she was wrong. She tried not to change her rhythm lest it scare him off, keeping to a leisurely pace as she veered off through the trees and on to the hockey field. Despite the chill of the night, her blood pulsed warmly inside her, fizzed in her ears in the silence. She was having trouble not turning around.

What was he expecting of her, she wondered. She had a dread feeling that she would make the wrong move and lose him, kill the moment. She strode up towards the goal, the goal that only yesterday she had been defending as the man looked on. All that seemed like light years away. When she had still been Tristan's girl. The body that Tristan wanted to fuck. Another notch on his bedpost.

She thought again of Tristan's dick, his smooth pale dick like a swatch of silk in her hand. The way he'd presented himself to her. He thought he was sex on a stick, that guy. He didn't know the meaning of the word.

She shrugged off her coat and scarf, began to unbutton her shirt and then grew impatient and pulled it up over her head, tossing it to the ground beside her. Before she could tell herself otherwise, she had turned to face the man. He was only steps behind her now, his face contorted with longing. Full on, she could see now that he wasn't old enough to be her father, but must have had a good fifteen years on her. She held out her hand. He looked at it, and she could almost hear his brain ticking over.

'It's OK,' she whispered. 'I won't tell. It'll be our little secret.'

He scrunched his face up, as if weighing up her words, deciding whether he could trust her. 'Not here,' he whispered finally, glancing up at the moon, as if it were some all-seeing eye.

'Then where?'

He pointed back in the direction of his shed.

'No.' She stepped forwards and encircled his wrist with her hand, pulling him over towards a mass of bushes. Her coat and shirt remained on the grass behind her.

He took off his donkey jacket as they reached the flower bed and made to throw it down on the earth, but she pushed his hand away.

'No,' she said again, still more forcefully. And then she slipped off her remaining clothes and shoes and laid herself down.

He stood looking over her. 'Are you sure?' he said.

She nodded. 'Absolutely. Now just fucking get on with it, will you, I'm freezing my tits off.'

He snorted, repressing a laugh. 'Bossy little madam, aren't you?'

She smiled. 'Just take your clothes off. Or do I have to do it for you?' At this she sat up and lunged for him, pulling him back down on to her by his tired brown sweater and then pulling it up over his head. Beneath it was an equally worn navy T-shirt that she tore off him too. In the half-dark she could see the fur of his chest, of his shoulders. She pressed her hands against it, the fuzz of it. It felt comforting. There was a ripe smell about him: sweat and onions and nicotine and lust, and that comforted her too. There was something so irrepressibly male about it.

She lay back, spread her legs. 'Lick me,' she commanded.

He smiled, as if he still couldn't quite believe his luck, and then brought his face down to her. She arched her back as she felt his tongue jab inside her, once, twice, and then plunge right into her and stay there, exploring the walls of her. The melting feeling returned.

'Don't stop,' she murmured. 'Just don't fucking stop.'

He came up for air, and she saw the lower half of his face glistening. Straining upwards, she licked his chin and around his mouth, her tongue rasping against his beard growth, tasting her own slightly sour juices on his skin. Then she lowered herself to the ground again, and pulled his head back down. This time his tongue flicked at the nub of her clitoris, and she felt herself jerk like a puppet, at the mercy of new forces. It was uncomfortable, almost unbearable, and yet she didn't want it to end. Her hands opened and closed like avid claws, convulsively, tearing up the soil beneath her. Her legs spasmed peculiarly, almost comically. A couple of times she came close to pushing him away from her but realised she couldn't. She was on the verge of tears, even while she was shouting out with joy.

'I want you inside me,' she said, not knowing where she found it in herself to order this grown man about. He raised his head, smiled down at her, then pulled her legs wide apart and placed his clenched fist up against her pussy.

'Relax,' he whispered.

She smiled. 'I am,' she said. 'Perfectly relaxed.'

He unfurled his hand, pushed three fingers inside her and waited, watching her face. She had half-closed her eyes now, and her head was pushed back, chin jutting up, in a swoon. 'More,' she whispered. 'Go further. Harder.'

Soon his entire hand was inside her, and he stopped again, reading her face for a signal. She looked up at him, remembering the care with which he handled his plants, the way he caressed their leaves with his fingertips, urging them to trust him. She trusted him. She nodded.

He began to rock his hand gently inside her, moving slightly from one side and then to the other. She was still now, palms pressed down against the soil, breath stopped. And then a flood tide opened within her, and the contractions started, and for a time she lost all contact with the earth beneath her.

When she woke up he was gone, but he'd draped his coat over her, and her own. It was still only half-light, and sounds from the road were scant, so she guessed she'd only been asleep a matter of minutes, perhaps an hour at the most.

She sat up, pulled away the covering and looked at her bare legs, at her lips still glistening in the dawn, at the smearing of blood on her thighs, mingling with the crust of mud. She lay back, just for a moment, and felt the dewy soil against her skin.

'You dirty, dirty girl,' she said and laughed.

She stood up and got dressed. When she passed the shed, the door was closed and the storm lamp was out. She folded his jacket and placed it on the ground outside, wondering whether he would be back to watch her the following week. Then she remembered the hockey season was over.

'Goodbye,' she shouted as she made for the gate, not waiting for a reply.

Candy Wong's short stories have appeared in numerous Wicked Words collections. She also writes as Carrie Williams and her first novel, *The Blue Guide*, is published by Black Lace in August 2007.

Cooking Lessons
Teresa Noelle Roberts

I studied the ingredients that Zak had assembled on the counter. Tomatoes in a bowl, already peeled and chopped. Peanuts. Two kinds of chillies, one in a can, the other soaking in water. Allspice berries. Small, hard reddish seeds labelled ANNATTO BERRIES. Cloves. Cinnamon sticks. Olive oil flavoured with garlic.

And a bar of bittersweet chocolate.

I started singing, 'One of these things is not like the other . . .'

Zak laughed. 'I thought we'd make Mexican chicken with red mole. The chocolate is the secret ingredient. Trust me.'

'We' was being generous. This was my third time having dinner at Zak's. The first two times, he made the kinds of meals you'd pay big money for in a restaurant and I helped by chopping vegetables and doing other things that didn't require much in the way of real cooking skills. 'Of course I trust you. You are the master chef and my guide in all things culinary.'

'Stop. You're making me blush.' He was smiling, and while he did turn a bit pink, it was more what I'd call a flush, the slight change in colour that shows a fair-skinned redhead is feeling good about life.

From that brief description, you probably picture freckles and light eyes and a full name along the lines of Zachary O'Connell. Actually his name is Itzak Meyer. Amend your mental picture to include brown eyes, ivory skin with a warm undertone and thick curly hair a deep, rich red that you'd never call auburn or carrot. Add a Caravaggio saint's sensual mouth, which seems out of place with a tall, big-boned Eastern European build and a face created to study the Kabbalah by flickering candlelight. I'd fallen for him while watching him eat a particularly decadent chocolate-marzipan torte at a mutual friend's party. The luscious mouth and blissful expression sparked my interest; watching the passion and precision with which he cooked stoked it. He liked things hot and spicy and complex. This I took as a good sign.

There was one problem. Zak's culinary boldness didn't extend into other areas. Some guys move too fast. He was the other sort, the guy who's clearly interested, but so determined not to be pushy that a girl ends up having to take matters into her own hands. That was my plan for the evening. But I didn't want to rush things either. For one thing, a sauce that combined chocolate and spices was just too intriguing to miss. I wasn't the cook that Zak was, but I liked good food.

'So, molé,' I said, hoping it sounded casual. 'Where do we start?' I put my hand on his arm, looked up at him and leaned in more than was necessary. He echoed my movement so we were definitely in each other's personal space. A little closer and we'd be wrapped around each other.

So far so good.

'Well, first we taste-test the chocolate.' Zak popped a square into his mouth, then broke me off a piece. I could almost see him thinking through how to give it to me. I was delighted when he held it up so I could eat it from his hand.

Naturally, I took the bait. I made eye contact the whole time, nibbled the tips of his fingers as I took the chocolate, and then licked them to make sure I got any melted bits. It was fine bittersweet chocolate, not that I would have expected anything less from Zak, but it didn't taste nearly as good as he did. By the time his fingers were clean, I felt as melted as the chocolate had been.

He made an exaggerated 'cool me down' fanning motion. 'Oh yeah, that's good. And the chocolate wasn't bad either. Where were we?'

'We'd just gotten started.'

I hoped he'd pick up on the suggestion, but he was either clueless or hungry and determined to make this meal. I opted to believe the latter. 'We need to roast the peanuts and the spices, and then grind them. If you'll chop the chillies that are soaking, I'll start that.' I don't think I imagined that he sounded a little flustered, or that he was a little more flushed.

The peanuts went into the oven, a pile of spices into a dry skillet. Meanwhile, I went to work on the chillies, removing the seeds and stems and chopping what was left into fine pieces. They were ancho chillies, not super-hot, but with a rich, smoky, raisiny aroma that the chopping released. From the stove, the fragrance of spices and nuts filled the air, tempting my taste buds and tickling my nose. I could recognise clove and peppercorns, but roasting peanuts smelled surprisingly wonderful, and other aromas – annatto and allspice, I guessed – added complexity. Delicious.

Zak came over behind me. 'You can do big chunks,' he said, leaning over my shoulder. 'We'll be putting them into the food processor.'

I set the knife down and leaned back as if stretching, knowing this would bring me into contact with his body. He didn't pull away, so I wrapped my arms around him and cupped his butt, despite the awkward angle. 'Thanks for inviting me over.'

He slipped his arms around me. 'My pleasure.' The contact was lovely, but not enough. Feeling him against me, I immediately flashed to how wonderful it would be if I were leaning on the counter and he was pushing into me from behind, hitting all the right spots, gripping my hips decisively as he moved. I wriggled a little at the delicious image and he pulled me closer in a way that suggested his thoughts were heading in a similar direction.

Unfortunately at that point we both noticed the aroma of spice was getting more intense. I'd already learned from an earlier adventure in Indian cuisine with Zak that spices burn easily, so I wasn't offended when he wheeled around to pull the skillet from the heat. Disappointed, but not offended. 'That was close. The peanuts should be ready now too.' He pulled them from the oven and set the tray on the counter. 'We should let it all cool before we grind it.'

'Good,' I said. 'That'll give us a few minutes.' And then I kissed him.

When you catch someone off-guard with a kiss, you expect a second or so of confusion – more than that and you should probably stop kissing and start apologising. I figured Zak, being shy, might need a little extra time before he relaxed.

He didn't. He took me in his arms and returned the kiss as if he'd been waiting his whole life to do so. The sheer force of his pent-up desire came through on his lips, his hands on my back and ass, the heat of him against me. And I don't mean that in a he-hadn't-had-a-date-lately sort of way. This felt personal, and it burned straight into me, hot as chillies and sweet as chocolate. I buried my fingers in his hair, tried to pull him even closer. I didn't realise that I'd instinctively started grinding my pelvis against his until I felt him getting hard against me.

I was wet already, and that caused flooding. There were about a thousand things I wanted to say to him, but that would have meant using my mouth for something besides kissing. And there were about a thousand things I wanted to do and with him, all crowding into my head at once (frankly, some of them had already been camped out there for a while), but they could all wait a while so we could enjoy the moment.

He didn't rush, either. He kissed with the patience of a man who made bread and the passion of one who'd drive a hundred miles to get the perfect ingredient, and I realised that what seemed like caution might have been a matter of waiting for the right moment. He wasn't doing anything but holding me and kissing me, not attempting to rip off my clothes or anything, but the word *kissing* covers a lot of territory. Nibbles and licks and sucking my tongue and lower lip. Gentle mouth-caresses and fierce kisses that threatened to devour me whole. And I was giving back as good as I got. By the time we had to pause for air, he was rock-hard against me and I was trembling.

He let me unbutton his shirt, showing off a broad, furred chest, but when I reached for his fly, he took my hand and gently but firmly moved it away. 'Oh no,' he said with a wonderfully evil smile, 'we need to finish making the molé. But first . . .' He didn't let go of my wrist. Instead, he put it behind my back.

Such a small gesture, but it had such a weight of possibilities behind it, possibilities I hadn't even really considered where quiet, seemingly shy Zak was concerned. Vanilla is a lovely flavour, but it's not my favourite one. I drew a sharp breath, both delighted and excited, and felt my knees go a little weak.

Catching my reaction, he grinned approvingly. 'Just as I thought,' he said. Then he used his free hand to unbutton my blouse with a deftness that up until a few minutes ago would have surprised me.

He definitely wasn't shy or overly cautious. Zak had been stalking his prey, and I'd walked right up to him thinking he was harmless. I was wrong.

Lucky me.

My breasts are of the smallish, perky variety, so my red lace bra was more decorative than structural. Even one-handed, Zak was able to move it out of the way easily, baring my nipples. He traced the ring in the left one with one finger and was rewarded with a sharp, pleasured intake of breath. 'Now that's a nice surprise.'

'Glad you like.' I don't think I was talking above a whisper.

'Oh, yes.' He bent down, took the ringed nipple in his mouth.

Damn, that man had a clever tongue. And he didn't make the mistake of assuming that because I was pierced I must like rough handling from the word go. He was exquisitely delicate, even while the firm grip on my wrist promised that this would not always be the case. It made me writhe, took me to that place where even a light touch on my clit would have pushed me over the edge.

He didn't do it. Instead, he reduced me to the point of gibbering, weak-kneed idiocy, and then drew the bra back up over my nipples. 'More later,' he said, again with that evil grin.

'Do we have to finish the sauce now?' I was whining, I admit.

'It won't take much longer. Then we'll have a few hours while the chicken marinates – and another hour while it cooks.'

That put us eating dinner at about ten o'clock. I'd do something like that by mistake, from boldly setting forth to cook something without reading through the recipe all the way or something equally foolish, but Zak wouldn't. 'You planned this.'

'Hell, yes, I did. I've had my eye on you since the night we met. But you screwed up my time-table – I was going to start things once the chicken was marinating. And I'm still going to, because otherwise we'll have to order out.' It was clear from his tone that ordering out would be a defeat for him. But he didn't let go of me as he said it.

'So let's get cooking!'

Reluctantly, we peeled apart from each other. Not too far, though. It's hard to cook with one person holding the other's wrist, so he did let go eventually, but we kept in contact as much as we could.

We whirred the peanuts in the food processor, then puréed the anchos I'd chopped and the canned chipotles, throwing the tomatoes in with them. The roasted spices and a cinnamon stick went into a spice grinder, filling the kitchen with an even headier aroma as they were reduced to powder. We kissed over the grinder, inhaling the fragrance and setting ourselves on fire again.

Zak poured olive oil into a skillet and turned up the heat. When the oil was steaming, he poured in the purée and spices, then stirred in the peanuts.

Everything had smelled good to begin with. As it heated together, the perfume became even more extraordinary, and the garlic in the olive oil added its own notes to the olfactory symphony. 'Get the chocolate,' he said. His voice had such a husky quality to it that he might have been saying, 'Get the condoms' or even 'Get the whip.'

I did.

He let me stir in the melting chocolate, the almost-black streaks spreading out, then turning the brilliant red sauce to burgundy. 'Taste,' Zak said, practically making it an order.

Explosions on my tongue. Smoky and complex and spicy, yet not overly hot. The chocolate had melded with the many other components, adding depth and a hint of subtle sweetness. If I hadn't helped make the sauce, I wouldn't have guessed chocolate was the source of that dark, rich undertone. 'Oh my God. This is so good. How come I've never had this before?'

'Stick with me, baby,' he said, doing a remarkably bad Bogart imitation, 'and you'll get to taste a lot of new things.' He accompanied that with a lovely little hip-grind against me.

I don't know how we got the chicken into the marinade without spilling something major, because we certainly weren't being careful.

As soon as it was safely in the fridge, clothing began to fly. My bra ended up in the sink with the dirty dishes, but I failed to care, being more interested in getting a good look at Zak. I'd expect a hedonistic gourmet cook to have a little belly rather than six-pack abs, and I was right, but he looked fine to me: muscled arms and good, broad shoulders, nice legs, not a runner's but not a couch potato's either. And any woman who complains about a paunch when there's all that, an attractive face, a creative and sensual mind and an erection you could use as a flagpole doesn't know when she has it good.

He lifted me up and set me on a corner of the kitchen counter. I took the hint and opened my legs, resting one foot on the counter to give him better access, and wriggled down a bit to put my crotch on a better level. I don't fantasise about men kneeling at my feet in a high-heeled-vixen-with-a-whip sense – my kinks are more on the other side of the fence – but there are certain lovely things one can do from that position. When he knelt down I shuddered with anticipation, already knowing that Zak had a talented tongue, patience and a bit of an oral fixation.

He started by kissing and nibbling my mound, not touching the slick lips or straining, swollen clit below. Just enough to inflame me, just enough to send hot, sweet bolts of desire surging through me. I gripped the edge of the counter and squirmed against him. Now he let one finger trace each of my lips, feeling their plumpness, as he kissed my inner thighs, followed the crease of the joint with his tongue. 'Tease,' I panted. He laughed deep in his throat but didn't say anything. He had better things to do with his mouth.

Just when I thought I couldn't take any more teasing, he let his tongue go where his fingers had been, licking along my slippery outer lips, making me shiver and croon. Little, delicate, entirely controlled licks, reaching ever closer to my most sensitive areas, but not actually touching them. Delicious, but not enough, so far from being enough. My hand closed in his hair. I meant to pull him closer and end the glorious frustration, but there was an almost imperceptible hesitation on his part. I got the point – that he was doing things on his own timetable, not mine – and contented myself with playing with his flame hair.

At last he relented and turned his attention to my clit. Focused, precise and intense as he had been in his teasing, he began to lick.

After the long build-up, I exploded almost instantly. I felt it all over my body, radiating out from my clit until every bit of me, including, I swear, my hair, was tingling and shimmering. I bucked against his face, gripping the edge of the counter with one hand and his shoulder with the other and moaning.

When Zak stood up again, he had to catch me – I was so limp I was ready to slide off the counter. I nestled against his chest, playing idly with the curly pelt there, catching my breath. I even wrapped my legs around him to hold him closer.

That was what made us realise that the counter would be useful again, this time as something to brace against.

Before I had time to wonder how I'd get to my now-distant purse without letting go of Zak, he pulled a condom out of a nearby drawer with a flourish, like a magician pulling a rabbit out of a hat. I was almost too eager, clumsy as I rolled it onto his straining penis. His cock was thick, hot under my hands. It jumped with anticipation at my first touch, and my cunt jumped in response.

There would be time to play with this pretty

thing later, to lick and suck and swallow. Right now, though, I just guided him to my pussy lips and said, 'Now. Please.'

I expected him to tease me, to take his time as he had before, but he drove it straight home, lifting me up with the force of the thrust. His eyes darkened to an unlikely espresso as his pupils widened. I wrapped my arms and my legs around him and lost my mind.

More bone-melting kisses. I couldn't move all that much in that position, but he made up for it, driving fiercely into me, moving me against him with his strong hands. I did what I could, moving my pelvis in a small circle (I knew those jazz dance classes would come in handy for something!) and tightening myself to grip at him. Pretty soon my pussy set up a rhythm of its own, and it was a good thing I didn't need to concentrate on it because I no longer could.

My last semi-coherent thought was, I hope he doesn't mind being scratched, as I clawed convulsively at his back. Then everything was dark red, red as molé sauce, behind my eyelids and I startled the remote part of myself that could still care with the insane-wildcat noises I made as I came. Zak grunted and began moving even faster, keeping me locked in ecstasy as he drove towards his own climax.

He cried out, wordless and triumphant, lifting me away from the counter so he supported all my weight as he came. Our mouths locked again, and we sank to the floor together, too spent to crawl somewhere more comfortable.

Zak's first words were, 'And that's only the appetiser. I think we'll need to rest a little before the entrée, though, and maybe make it to the bedroom.' He was grinning like a fool – not that I blamed him, because I was too – but I had a feeling that he was serious about this being just the beginning of a long and very interesting night.

I made a happy-animal noise and snuggled against him, breathing deeply. The kitchen smelled like spices, chocolate and passion.

Teresa Noelle Roberts's short stories have appeared in several Wicked Words collections. She is also one half of Sophie Mouette, author of the Black Lace Novel *Cat Scratch Fever*.